Power Play

Erica Frost

Published by Erica Frost, 2023.

POWER PLAY

First edition. January 13, 2023.

Copyright © 2023 Erica Frost.

ISBN: 979-8223876311

Written by Erica Frost.

Table of Contents

Power Play
New Adult Hockey Enemies To Lovers Romance

By: Erica Frost

Foreword

My Small Town Bad Boy Enemy Becomes My College Lover

I'd been throwing myself into my college studies to distract myself from heartbreak when my hometown enemy, brother of my best friend, boy who had taken every opportunity to tease me over the years, suddenly wanted to be my boyfriend.

His name is Harry and he's a couple of years older than me. After he gets kicked off his precious hockey team, he comes to me to try and help salvage his reputation. Frankly, I'm ready to see him suffer, but I have problems of my own.

My ex comes back into the picture and makes college a living hell. I decide to take Harry's offer; it might help me get back at my ex. But then something bad happens; I start falling in love.

Power Play

Chapter One

Angel

I walked through the Met as I did any other day. I wasn't sure why we called it the Met. I guess it was just something that was passed down from generation to generation and the meaning got lost somewhere along the way. The sun was shining, the world seemed fresh, and for once I was actually in a good mood. There was a spring in my step as I had just gotten a great grade from a test that I thought I was going to flunk for sure, so I felt as though I could take on the world and maybe, just maybe, things were going to change for the better.

The campus was beautiful, with its historic buildings giving the place a sense of history. There was a vast area of grass outside the library, where I was heading, and because it was a sunny day people were enjoying the weather. Some were just lazing around, while others were throwing a football or playing soccer. I breathed in deeply. I felt at home.

I was eager to get into the library as the stack of books was weighing down my shoulder. I approached the doors, but just as I did so I heard someone shouting my name. I turned around to see Phil, a guy in one of my classes. We'd worked together on a project a while back and he carried the burden because I had been in a bad way at the time. I smiled as he approached. He was fresh-faced and wore a charming smile.

"Hey Angel, I haven't seen you around much since we did that project together. How are you doing?" he asked.

"I'm fine, just trying to keep my head above water and make sure that I don't fall behind," I replied.

"That's no way to live. Surely you didn't just come to college to study?" he asked with a sarcastic twinkle in his eyes. I chuckled a little.

"There will be plenty of time for partying when I'm done with exams."

"I don't know, sometimes these things only happen once and then they pass you by. Anyway, look, I know you're busy with studying and things, but I wondered if you wanted to get a coffee sometime?"

I knew that he was attracted to me. It had been evident when we'd worked together, but the question still took me by surprise. Jeri, my best friend, would have rolled her eyes and wondered how I managed to catch the attention of all these guys. To be honest, I wasn't sure. It wasn't as though I was doing it intentionally. My heart seized with tension when he asked the question. I wish I had the courage to say yes, but the words wouldn't come. Even though I told myself I was ready to date again, I still couldn't quite bring myself to make that final step.

"That's a really sweet offer Phil, but I'm really swamped with studying at the moment. Maybe when I get a chance?" I said.

He pressed his lips together and smiled. I could tell that he was disappointed. He walked away and I inhaled deeply, wondering if I had just made a mistake. It had been a while now since I had suffered the worst heartbreak of my life. I was over most of the pain, but some of it still lingered and I wasn't quite ready to throw myself back into the dating world again. The thought was daunting and maybe I was wasting the best years of my college life, but I couldn't help but worry the worst was going to happen again.

I tried to push the thoughts out of my mind and head into the library. Burying myself in studying always worked to help distract me, but before I could reach the door I was called back yet again, this time by Jeri. I turned around, a little aggrieved, but that feeling quickly vanished when I saw the look on her face.

"What's wrong?" I asked.

"Oh Angel, you wouldn't believe what's happened. Harry has been kicked off the team!"

She looked stricken, but I had no sympathy. I scoffed and let out a dry laugh.

"Oh, is that all?" I said.

"Angel! Come on, you know how important hockey is to him. This is a disaster! And you wouldn't believe what they're saying about him. You have to have some feeling, he's my brother after all."

"Yes, exactly, the same brother who used to tease me for being a nerd just because I liked studying, the same brother who took every opportunity to needle me whenever I was around. If you ask me, he had this coming," I said bitterly. The memories of youth were still strong, as were the feelings Harry had caused. He was a couple of years older than us. When we were young that had felt like an eternity. Jeri and I had been neighbors, so naturally we had been best friends all through high school, and the only bad thing about that had been that I had to put up with Harry. We even ended up going to the same college together, although thankfully I saw less of him here than I did at home.

"We were just kids then. Everyone does stupid things when they're kids. It's not fair what they're saying about him. I feel really bad. I don't know what to do."

"I don't know Jeri, but whatever he's done I'm sure it's something he's guilty of. I know that you've always worshiped your brother, but he's never been very nice to me, so you won't get much pity from me."

"I know you're still upset over what Tommy did-" Jeri started. I didn't give her a chance to finish.

"This has nothing to do with Tommy," I said in a harsh voice, far louder than I wanted to. I cringed as I noticed people looking at me, and my cheeks flushed red. I made an effort to keep my voice low. "This goes back way before Tommy. You know how Harry used to treat me, hell, how he used to treat everyone!"

"That's not fair. He's not that bad. Sure, he was a jerk when we were younger, but most guys are."

"It was bad enough when we were kids, but there have been moments through high school as well. I know you don't like talking about this, but he's not the guy you think he is."

"No, he's not the guy you think he is," Jeri said. "I know he's not perfect, but he's always looked out for me. I just wish you could see that."

"I can only see the way he's treated me, Jeri. I don't even know why you'd come to me with this. You know there has always been tension between us."

"Because you're my best friend. You're the only one I can turn to about this stuff."

I heard the desperation in her voice. I was torn between my love for her and my hatred of Harry. Eventually the love won out.

"Okay," I sighed. "How about you just tell me how this started. What's Harry done?"

"It's not about what he's done. It's about what they say he's done."

"Which is?" I asked, placing extra emphasis on the word. Jeri was stricken with grief, and I honestly thought that she was going to collapse in tears. I had never understood the relationship she had with Harry. She was the only one who ever gave him any credit, and I guess it must have been a holdover from their childhood when she worshiped the ground that he walked on. All I knew was that he was a bully and he had never shown me any kindness.

"They said he got in a fight, that he attacked someone."

"Isn't that just part of hockey? Or have they cracked down on the rules now?"

"No, not in the game. Out of the game! They say it happened on campus, but he wouldn't do anything like this. You know he wouldn't!"

I remained silent, for I knew no such thing. I felt bad for Jeri though, she was clearly sensitive about the whole thing, but there wasn't much I could do to make her feel better. I also didn't understand why she was so upset.

"It's just a fight though, right?"

"No, it's more than that. They've kicked him off the team! He's not going to play hockey anymore."

Suddenly it dawned on me why she was so upset. I should have seen it earlier really. It was the only thing that would have inspired such an intense reaction from her. Practically the only thing Harry had going for him was that he was an ace on the ice. All his life he'd had one dream and one dream only; to go pro and light up the world with his name, earning trophies and glory along the way. He'd always been smart enough to get the grades needed to pass academically, but his true focus was hockey. Without that he was nothing.

"Will you come and see him with me? Please. I know things are awkward between you, but he's not the same person he was when he was younger. He's changed, believe me, and I know he didn't do this," Jeri said.

"Are you sure?" I asked. I had to ask the question, even if Jeri would hate me for it.

"I know he didn't. Now are you going to come and help me? Do you remember all I've done for you since Tommy? Who was there to dry your tears? Who was there to comfort you and tell you it was going to be alright? Who was there when all you wanted to do was rant and rave and scream and shout? I was," she pointed to her chest as she said this. "I've always been there for you, Angel. I've never let you down, not once, so I'm just asking you for this one favor, just one. That's all. Is that so much to ask?"

Shame filled my heart. Of course, I remembered all she had done for me. Jeri was the most loyal person in my life, and I don't know where I would have been without her. After Tommy did what he did all I wanted was for the ground to open up and swallow me whole, but Jeri was there to remind me that I still had a life to live. She comforted me like a mother and protected me like a father. As much as I hated to admit it in this moment, I owed her. So, I agreed to go with her and see Harry, the man who had tormented me as a child, the man whose name still caused my stomach to clench whenever I heard it.

Frankly it didn't surprise me to hear that he had been in a fight, and unlike Jeri, I didn't believe his innocence. As far as I was concerned, he deserved whatever punishment they gave to him. I walked a couple of steps behind Jeri to hide the smile on my face.

Chapter Two

Angel

Harry lived in a nicer dorm than we did. That was due to his position as a senior, while we were lowly sophomores. It also helped that he was a star of the hockey team, although, if what Jeri said was any indication then it seemed as though those days were over. He must have done something drastic to get himself cut, which surprised me because hockey had always been his life. There had never been anything else. He was a mean son of a bitch, especially to me as a kid, but on the ice, I guess that counted for something. I always felt bad for Jeri because she had been the neglected child. Their parents were nice, but since Harry was the eldest and he had a passion for hockey they poured all their energy into supporting him, leaving Jeri to fend for herself most of the time. I guess that's why we gravitated to each other. Jeri used to stay with us a lot while they were off taking Harry to hockey camps or to games all across the country so that he could get his name known. Jeri was looking for a family and since I didn't have a sister, I was looking for someone to spend time with as well, it was just a shame that she came with the baggage of her jerk brother. When we were little, we used to joke that she should just get adopted by my parents and we could be sisters properly, but that never happened.

I guess now that I'm older I can see why her parents put so much effort into Harry's hockey life. As much as I hated to admit it, he was good. I had seen more matches than I cared to admit, and I had cheered begrudgingly as he won championship after championship for our school, and by all accounts he had carried that form with him into college. He was destined for the top and, after all the effort and money and time his parents had put into his hockey education, it would have been waste for him to not make it pro, but if he was kicked off the team that could scupper all his chances. I could see why Jeri was worried, and

I tried to remind myself that I was doing this for her rather than for Harry.

Harry's dorm was located in the original building of the college, the oldest and most prestigious place there was on campus. The walls breathed respect and there was always a sense of history whenever I came here. There was a small library that housed the oldest books and was used by the highest honored students as a private place where they could work away from the rabble. As the college expanded and grew, new buildings were added across the campus, including a new library that could provide enough space for the entire student body, so to be allowed to study in this building was a privilege indeed. We walked up the wide staircase and passed portraits of all the important people in the college's history. To me, they were just faces of strangers, but once upon a time, they would have walked the same path I did. I wonder whether they ever thought of themselves as doing anything important. I knew my portrait would never be hanging on a wall. I just hoped to get through college with my grades intact. It had been a rollercoaster of a year. They had suffered after what happened with Tommy, but I had managed to focus and pull them back up. If I could maintain momentum, then I could go back home feeling proud and really use college as a springboard to the rest of my life, but I couldn't shake the feeling that something was going to knock me off my equilibrium.

The hallway was long, stretching out into what seemed like an eternity. There were more paintings hanging on the walls, and many of the rooms were closed. Unlike my own dorm there was a sense of stately respect here, while my dorm was chaotic. The walls were made of old stone, although I didn't get a chance to examine them too closely because Jeri was walking quickly. I had to admire the devotion she showed Harry, which I personally thought was entirely undeserved, but I suppose that in her family, she either had to fall in line with her parents in their adulation of Harry or be alone. It was a shame things had to be this way, but I guess that's the way things go. Sometimes I was glad I didn't have a brother. I think they're more trouble than they're worth.

We reached his dorm and Jeri knocked on the door. There was no answer. She knocked again, and there was still no answer.

I rolled my eyes.

"Come on Jeri, he obviously doesn't want to see us so we might as well leave," I said.

"I'm not going anywhere," she replied in a terse voice. "He needs me and I'm not just going to ignore him." She turned back to the door. This time instead of knocking she hammered her fists against it, breaking the gentle silence that lingered around the dorm. "Harry I'm coming in!" she yelled. I cringed at the thought of everyone listening to us. She pushed her weight against the door, turning the handle, and I guess it was a good thing it was unlocked otherwise I was quite sure that Jeri would have rammed the door down until it was nothing but debris.

We entered into a dimly lit room. The walls were plastered with posters of hockey players. There was a cabinet filled with trophies and awards, although I knew this was only a small selection of Harry's accolades. In his house, there was basically a room dedicated to his trophies. A window was slightly open, offering a gentle breeze that helped to cut away from the mustiness of the room. Unlike our dorms Harry and people like him had the privilege of enjoying privacy. Sharing with Jeri wasn't much of a big deal considering we had been close our entire lives, but there were times when it was a drag to have to share a room with someone. Harry never had to deal with that. It always amazed me how athletes were given such special treatment compared to the rest of us. I get that he worked hard to get to where he wanted to be, but he was treated like a god.

However, he didn't look much like a god at the moment. He was prostrate on the bed with his arms resting behind his head, gazing up at the ceiling with a glazed look upon his face. He didn't move when we entered, he didn't even react. He just kept staring, as though he was frozen in time.

"Harry what is this all about?" Jeri asked, marching around to stand beside his bed. I remained by the door, leaning against the frame.

"It doesn't matter," he replied quietly, his words hollow and empty, as though he had lost all hope of speaking.

"Yes, it does. Come on, we can fight this. I want to help you. Angel and I are both here. You don't have to go through this alone. How could they throw you off the team? It doesn't make any sense. You're the star player!"

I flinched when Jeri said that he had both of us to support him, but I didn't say anything figuring that it would only serve to make Jeri angry. I folded my arms across my chest.

"They made their decision. I have to live with it," Harry said.

"But that doesn't make any sense! We don't just have to live with it. You deserve to be on the team, Harry. Why did they even throw you out?"

"It doesn't matter," Harry said, this time with iciness in his voice, although he still didn't take his gaze off the ceiling. "I get what you're trying to do Jeri, but there's nothing you can do. I have to deal with this. There isn't any going back."

"But... but what are Mom and Dad going to say? What about how hard you've worked? They can't just throw you off the team," Jeri said. But they could, and they had.

"I don't know what's going to happen. I need to figure things out for myself. I need to think."

"There must be something I can do," Jeri said. "Maybe I can petition the coaches or something. I could go around campus and take a poll. I bet if we asked people, they would all vote to keep you on the team."

Harry smirked, but it was a gesture devoid of any humor. "You could ask a million people to get me back on the team, but unless it's anyone who matters, then it's not going to make a difference. They don't want me, Jeri, not the players and not the coach. It's over."

I could tell that Jeri wanted to fight against it, but what was the point when Harry himself had given up? Those two words, 'it's over,' had such a finality to them that it was almost depressing. Harry wasn't forthcoming about why exactly he had been kicked off the team, but it must have been something serious if he wasn't even willing to fight against the decision. There was a moment where I almost pitied him for what he was going through. He looked so lost and alone, but then I remembered the way he used to tease me when I was younger and any sympathy I had for him vanished. It was Jeri I felt sorry for the most. I saw her standing there, looking like a guardian angel over her brother, wanting to help him and save him, but he wouldn't let her. She was powerless. Throughout her life she had never really been able to affect Harry's world. She had supported him and cheered him on, but she had never been a part of it, not really. I could sense the yearning part of her that wanted so badly to fix this for him, to prove that she was a good sister, but it just wasn't going to happen.

Harry had made his decision, or at least he had accepted the decision that had been made against him.

"I can't believe you're just going to let this happen. I'm not. I'm going to help you Harry, whether you like it or not," Jeri said, stamping her foot and holding her arms rigidly by her side. She marched away from him and past me. Harry still didn't react, and I wondered how he could be so cold and callous even to his own sister. I took a moment to look at him staring at the ceiling and then I exited the room as well, closing the door behind me.

Jeri was leaning against the wall, head in her hands, sobbing desperately. Her shoulders shuddered and at the sound a few people opened their doors to see what the commotion was about. I glared at them, and they quickly retreated back into their solitude. I wasn't about to let them tell Jeri off for disturbing the peace. I put my arm around her shoulders and welcomed her into an embrace. It wasn't so long ago that our roles had been reversed and she was the one holding me.

"Hey, it's okay, it's okay," I cooed, trying to soothe her. I knew the words wouldn't make any difference; it was more a case of knowing that someone was there for her.

"It's not okay though, is it?" she said through a cascade of tears.

"You can't let yourself get upset because he's kicked off the team. That's his own problem and he's going to have to deal with it in his own way. I know you want to do more to help, but this is his decision and you're going to have respect that," I said. "But it's not going to change your life. It's not you who has been banned from a team."

"That's not why I'm upset," she groaned, wiping her eyes and her nose, sniffing back the glistening sadness that poured over her face. "I'm not upset because he's been kicked off the team... at least that's not why I'm crying. I'm upset because he's not letting me help. All I want to do is take care of him and help him. We're supposed to be a family. It's what Mom and Dad would do if they were here, but he never sees me like that. I'm just his kid sister."

I nodded in understanding and caressed her shoulder. "I know, but he's always been the same. Harry hasn't ever seen either of us as women. We're just the girls whose pigtails he wants to pull to tease us. That's just the way he is. I know you don't like me speaking this way about him, but there's going to have to come a point where you just accept that he is the way he is," I said. I was trying to be sympathetic to her, but I didn't see that there was any point in her continuing this delusion. Unfortunately, her parents had done a real number on her and trained her into thinking that she had to win Harry's approval because he was the star of the family, but it was something that was never going to happen because he wasn't ever going to give that approval. Harry only cared about one thing and one thing only: himself. I suppose that's what happens when parents build their lives around their children though. I was trying to be pragmatic and hoped that it would be enough to finally pull Jeri out of this mindset, but it seemed as though she would rather double down and focus even more intensely on being the sister she thought she should be.

She took a deep breath and sniffed back tears. There was a raw determination on her face, and it almost scared me with how powerful it was.

"I'm going to help him whether he likes it or not. He might be willing to take this lying down, but I'm not. I don't care what he says. I'm going to help my brother. I'm going to make them take him back on the team because that's where he belongs. He's the star player and he's going to make it pro," she said it like it was a fact. That's what she and her parents had been telling themselves for so long. They had put all of this energy into Harry's hockey career, that they believed it was destiny for him to succeed. Given that I could observe the situation with a more objective eye I knew that not to be the case, and I was saddened that Jeri was willing to put herself through this for his sake. But I felt my heart swell with admiration for my friend as well. She was the kind of person who would put herself through hell for the sake of someone she loved. She had done the same for me, and I couldn't be disappointed that she would do the same for her brother, even though I didn't think he deserved it, because that was just the kind of person she was. She was special, and I was fortunate to have her in my life. I embraced her in a hug to show her that at least someone cared about her and appreciated her, although I couldn't quite bring myself to tell her that I thought this was a good idea.

Chapter Three

Angel

It had been almost a week since I had first learned the news that Harry had been kicked from the team. It didn't take long for word to spread all across campus. Hockey was a big deal, and for Harry to be kicked was something of a shock to everyone. Speculation was rife, especially because nobody knew exactly why he had been kicked out. The faculty had issued a statement citing that he had been suspended indefinitely from the team for misconduct, which was a vague term and if left everyone wondering exactly what happened. I was a sucker for a mystery, so I couldn't deny that a part of me wanted to know as well, even though I didn't care about hockey or particularly about Harry.

But I did care about Jeri, and she was taking it hard. I had witnessed plenty of phone calls from her parents, who were on at her all the time for information even though she had none to give. Harry wasn't forthcoming with them either, so Jeri was bearing the brunt of all their frustration. I had a window into what it was like to have her whole world revolve around her brother, and once again I felt sorry for her. She often cried when she got off the phone because she felt helpless, and her parents gave her the impression that she was never doing enough.

"But you are," I tried to reassure her. "You're doing way more than your fair share. I've said this before, but it's Harry's problem, and he's the one who should be dealing with this. You're not the one who has to put up with this crap, especially not from your folks."

"They're just annoyed that they can't do anything to help," Jeri said, wiping away her tears. "They've tried to get onto the Dean, but he says it's an internal matter and he can't release details because of privacy issues. It's like it's some kind of cult. People know what's happening, but nobody is talking, and I don't understand why. Why won't he tell me Angel?"

She looked at me with those desperate eyes of hers and I wished that I had something more to tell her, but I couldn't make Harry act differently, and I couldn't transform her parents into nicer people. I tried to offer her as much comfort as possible, and I tried to tell her the truth, even though she didn't appreciate it. Part of the problem was that she continued to put herself into this situation when she didn't need to, but she wouldn't back away. She was convinced there was more to this story, and she claimed she wasn't going to rest until she found out what it was. I wasn't entirely sure that there was anything more to the story. Things with sports teams were in fluctuation all the time and I assumed that maybe he had just lost his form, but since Harry had accepted the decision, I just saw it as something that happened and that was entirely irreversible.

The difficult thing though was that gossip around the campus was rife. Jeri had tried to talk to a lot of people, and they all had different stories. Some of them believe that Harry had been kicked off the team because they discovered that he was doping himself up to improve his performances. This was in fact something a lot of people believed because he was so good that it was almost easier to believe he was using drugs rather than that his skill level was so much higher than everyone else. But for all the bad things I could say about Harry, I could never say that he was a cheat. I'd witnessed him play since he was a kid, and he just had a gift. When he was on the ice, he looked natural, as though he was born to skate around and the truth is that he never had a need to dope.

Others thought that it was something other than hockey, that he had been involved in a crime like assault or rape. This was something that I didn't want to consider, but I couldn't entirely dismiss out of hand. I wasn't about to say that to Jeri of course because she might well have dissolved our friendship. There was a limit to how much I could say about Harry. I didn't like to think it of him, but he had always been mean to me and I know that doesn't necessarily mean that he's capable of assaulting someone, sexually or otherwise, but people change over the years and how do you know what someone is going to turn into? People wear masks all the time and you never get to see the truth of them unless they show you. I'd learnt that the hard way with Tommy. I thought he was the best guy around, but then, well, he wasn't.

Who knew what was going through Harry's mind? People changed as they got older, and he was always ready to throw down on the ice. Had the anger spilled over from the ice in his personal life? And if another student was involved, then it would make sense why the Dean wouldn't reveal what happened due to privacy issues. Harry was a strong guy, his body had been honed to peak perfection and if he lost control... well, I dreaded to think what might happen.

There were other theories floating around as well, things like he was match fixing and gambling on games, or that while he didn't do drugs, he was smuggling them between campuses whenever he played away games. Either way it must have been something bad because, usually, athletes got a lot of leeway when it came to misdemeanors, but what could Harry have done?

He never struck me as the type to take a risk that would jeopardize his prospects in hockey. It was his dream more than anyone else's, so I doubted that he would have been stupid enough to endanger his entire career, which made the whole thing stranger to me. Jeri spent more time with him, but she said all he did was lay in bed and stare at the ceiling. She was distraught by the way he was handling this, and I hated him for it because it was taking such a toll on her, and he didn't seem to care. The least he could do was tell his parents to stop being so hard on her. She gave him so much love, but in return she got nothing back. I had long gotten over the fact that he was mean to me, but I could never forgive him for being mean to her.

It reached the point where I just couldn't take it any longer. Jeri was like a dog with a bone, and she just wasn't letting this go, but without Harry's help she couldn't get anywhere with it. She returned to our room in tears frequently, either because someone had said something mean about her brother or because he had told her to stop what she was doing. One day she returned and told me that she had a massive row with him.

"He told me to leave it all alone and that I should get back to my studies. He said that I was wasting my time with him, but how can I be wasting my time when I'm only trying to help him? I don't understand why he's being so mean to me," she lamented as she threw herself down on her bed. I hated the way she was pushing herself to her limits, neglecting her college work for the sake of trying to fix this mess that Harry had gotten himself into and seemed content to wallow in, and I knew it wasn't going to stop because she wasn't listening to reason. The only one who could stop this was Harry. He needed to stop yelling at her and actually talk with her, so I needed to go to him. It wasn't something I would usually do because the less I had to do with him the better, but it was something I was prepared to do for Jeri's sake. She was my best friend, and she didn't deserve to be treated like this.

Chapter Four

Angel

Sometimes I wondered if it was a fact of life that men just had to treat the women in their lives badly, no matter what kind of relationship it was. It was strange how it had manifested itself though. Harry was angry with Jeri all the time, yet she still felt as though she needed to do all she could to help him, as though she had to prove to him that he could rely on her, despite knowing that he would never do the same if the situation was reversed. I know the situation is different because they're siblings while Tommy and I were dating, but I couldn't help but compare the two situations. Tommy had never been angry with me, at least not until the end. Sometimes I wish he had, because then, maybe I would have gotten out of things before they got too bad. No, Tommy was always charming and kind, putting on this performance as a compassionate soul who would never dare do anything to hurt me. He was a real sweetheart. Problem was, it was all an act, and it was an act he was trying on other girls.

Even now, when I thought of him, I still felt a knot of anger tighten in the pit of my stomach. I had worked so hard to get past the point where the matter was making me sick, and where I couldn't stop thinking about it, and I wished I could excise all memory of him from my soul like a malevolent tumor, but I feared that he was here to stay. Tommy, Harry, they were all the same. All they did was make our lives hell.

I marched across the Met and made my way to Harry's room, where he inevitably was because he never seemed to leave. I noticed a few guys whispering as I passed. It was no secret that I was best friends with Jeri, and they all knew that she was Harry's sister. I guess they might have thought that I knew more than I did. I wish that had been true.

I took a deep breath as I stood outside his door, composing myself to be alone with this man who had tormented me when he was a boy.

Over the years, I had engineered situations so that I never was alone with him if I didn't have to be. It helped that he was usually busy with something hockey related, and if there were ever parties or barbecues hosted at Jeri's house, I used to sequester myself away somewhere far from Harry so that he didn't have an opportunity to tease me again. So, the fact that I was going into his room alone was a big deal for me, and I had to summon all the courage I could muster.

I didn't bother announcing myself. I walked in brazenly, trying to make him see that I wasn't there to mince words. He tilted his head when I walked in and from the delayed shock on his face, I assume that he expected me to be Jeri. I stood in front of him and folded my arms across my chest. He sighed and looked back at the ceiling.

"So, Jeri was right, you really are just letting yourself waste away here," I said.

"What do you want, Angel?" he said bitterly. "Did Jeri send you to try and tell me to fight the good fight again?"

"No, she didn't send me at all. She doesn't know that I'm here. I'm actually here to talk about the way you're treating her."

Harry looked at me and twisted his face in confusion. "I'm not doing anything to her."

"You might not think you are, but you're being awful to her. Have you even said thank you for what she's doing?"

"I never asked her to do this," Harry said. There was a blank look in his eyes, but there was an edge to his voice that I found interesting.

"It doesn't matter. She's choosing to do this because she cares about you, and she wants to make things better. She thinks she can fix this situation. She's just trying to be a good sister."

"It can't be fixed. I've told her this."

"No, you've shouted that to her and demanded that she stop, but you haven't actually told her what's going on. You haven't explained why it can't be fixed, and clearly you haven't asked your parents to stop calling her and getting on at her about it either."

His face fell at this. "I didn't know they were calling her."

I glared at him. For a guy who was at college he could be tremendously stupid. "What did you think they were doing?" I asked, my voice so heavy with disbelief that it was more like a squeal. "If they can't get a hold of you, then they're going to go to her, and when she can't tell them what they want to know, they get annoyed with her. She's running herself ragged for you, Harry, and it's not fair."

"No, it's not, but like I said, I never asked her to do this."

"It doesn't matter if you asked her or not. The fact is that she's doing it, and you need to do something to fix it. You need to be there for her just like she's trying to be there for you."

"And do what?"

"I don't know! Tell her that you're grateful for the help she's given, explain to her why you're in this situation in the first place. Buy her some flowers for goodness' sake. Just do something to show that you appreciate her rather than treating her like she's some kind of annoyance."

"She's not an annoyance."

"That's how you're making her feel. I don't understand how you can be so good at reading a game of hockey, but so bad at reading people. Don't you get how much Jeri worships you? She would do anything for you. While you've been moping in here, she's been out on campus talking to people, trying to find out what happened, and if there's any way to fix it. She's had to deal with people spreading rumors about you and looking at her like she's a pariah for having you as a brother, and then when she comes to you for some solace, she's turned away and is told that she's not doing anything worthy of her time. It's not fair to her, Harry. Sometimes I don't think you've ever grown up from the boy who used to toss dirt at me and call me names."

"I wasn't that bad," he said, and once again my face was a picture of disbelief.

"Are you kidding me? Whenever I wore a pretty shirt, you called me a nerd. Whenever Jeri and I watched cartoons, you told us that we were stupid. You used to kick our toys away and act like we were nothing, just because we didn't like the same things you did. It's clear that you see the world in a very different way than I do, and maybe that's fine for the most part, but not when it comes to Jeri. I'm not going to stand by and watch you treat her like this. She's your sister. She loves you, and she's been breaking her back trying to make things better for you. You might not want to help yourself here, but you're going to have to be nicer to her because at the end of the day she's the only here who is trying to help you. It seems as though everyone else has turned their back on you, and if you keep treating Jeri like this, it's only a matter of time before she does the same, and then where will you be?"

I let the question linger in the air. Harry didn't say anything in response. He sighed again and closed his eyes.

"I'll keep it in mind," he said, and that was all he said. I shook my head in dismay about how hard it was for him to show any kind of emotion or empathy. I could feel my blood getting hotter so I turned on my heels and marched out of the room, hoping that something I said would lodge in his mind, otherwise Jeri would continue to suffer, and I couldn't abide that happening.

*

As I returned to my dorm, ready to try and get some studying done so that I could keep up with my classes, I tried to ignore all the guys who stared at me. Some of them began to approach me but I dodged them, assuming that they only wanted to speak to me to try and get any hidden information about Harry. I didn't want to talk about him or anything else. It was easier to remain alone. I didn't think there was a man out there who I could trust not to hurt me. I had begun to think that I was ready to date again, but perhaps it was too soon. My heart wouldn't be able to take another betrayal, and right now the only feelings in my heart were bitter ones because of Tommy and Harry.

God, I wish that my experiences with men had been happier ones.

Chapter Five

Harry

I had a lot on my mind when Angel left. There was shame in my heart as she reminded me of how I had reacted when I was younger. The truth is I regretted it. I could say that I didn't know better, but even at the time, I knew what I was doing was wrong. I used to see the way her lower lip trembled as she tried to hold back tears and I wondered why I kept teasing her, but I just couldn't seem to be able to stop. I had only ever felt assured of myself when I was on the ice, and now that had been taken away from me as well.

But Angel had definitely given me a lot to think about. I smirked when I thought about how confident she had been. She had certainly grown up a lot over the years, she was far from the timid girl that had always scurried away whenever she saw me. I guess it was a symbol of my luck that a beautiful girl like her was inherently upset with me. Her hair was as golden as the sun, her eyes were as blue as the ocean. She was the All-American beauty, and I'm not sure she actually understood how stunning she was. The light scent of her perfume lingered in the air, and it made me think about all I had sacrificed for hockey. All my life it had been my main focus. Everything else had been left in its wake. Girls had left me in tears, angry and bitter that they hadn't been able to push ahead of my first love, feeling as though they were my mistress instead of my girlfriend. My studies had only ever been average as well. I had always done the bare minimum to survive, at the behest of my parents as they had prioritized my skills at hockey.

And now it was all falling apart, as though my dream had been a bubble in my hands and I had squeezed it a little too firmly, causing it to pop. It was all over now. As much as I hated it, I knew there was no going back, but perhaps I had been too hard on Jeri. I was so angry and probably lashed out at her because she was the only one who bothered with me. I pinched the bridge of my nose and frowned, annoyed at myself for letting things get this far. My life had been bubbling along at a steady pace with little in the way of threat, but suddenly, it had turned upside down and I wasn't sure how to get it back the right way up.

All my life, things had been laid out for me in a certain order. From a young age, I had known that I wanted to be a hockey player. It was a natural truth of the universe, as much an inherent part of me as any of my organs. I never needed to go to a careers guidance counselor, and I never had to fear for my future. Hockey was my game, my destiny, but now I was faced with the fact that it might all be taken away from me, and I didn't know what I was going to do.

I had never been faced with this question before. There had been a few people along the way who had warned me that I should think about back up plans just in case hockey didn't work out, but I never gave it much thought. I felt alive on the ice in a way that I didn't feel anywhere else, so if I couldn't skate then I didn't want to do anything else.

But now perhaps I did, and I was going to need people like Jeri.

I sent her a quick message, telling her to meet me for a coffee. I strode out of my dorm. I'd shut myself away for the past week, so when I emerged, I felt like a vampire who rose from a coffin after centuries of slumber. When I made my appearance outside, I noticed people looking at me and whispering. I wasn't unused to getting their attention of course because, as the star hockey player, they were often ready with compliments and praise, or just a brief smile of appreciation. But this time, they looked at me with suspicion and intrigue, as though I was a specimen at a zoo, only there for their enjoyment. I knew the rumors must have been flying through college and I dreaded what they must have thought of me. I was their hero, but now I had fallen into the dirt, my reputation was in tatters, and there was nothing I could do to change their minds.

I held my head high and tried not to let myself get distracted by the murmurings as I passed, or the comments made behind hands raised to mouths. None of them knew the truth. None of them could know the truth.

*

Jeri was waiting for me as I arrived at the small café. She smiled when she saw me and gave me a quick hug. We grabbed a couple of drinks and intended to sit down, but as soon as I entered people were staring at us and neither of us wanted to endure that kind of atmosphere. When Jeri suggested that we take our drinks to go, I readily agreed and we ventured outside, following the path around campus. At least out here, the people were spread out more sparsely and we didn't have to be plagued by the constant attention.

"Jeri, I wanted to tell you that I'm sorry for the way I've treated you. I didn't mean to snap at you or anything. I've just been under a lot of pressure recently and it's been getting to me, as you can imagine," I said. I don't know why, but I've always found it difficult to apologize, as though the words get lodged in my throat, but I managed to fight the resistance. Jeri seemed to appreciate it. When we met, tension had lined her face, but now she seemed a little more relaxed.

"It's okay, Harry. I know this can't have been easy for you. I've just wanted to help, that's all."

"I know, and I'm sorry I haven't appreciated that help. I get what you're trying to do, and I am thankful for it, but you have to understand it's not a simple thing that can be fixed."

"But it can be fixed, right? I mean, there has to be something we can do. It can't just end here, like this."

I shrugged, thinking about the conversation I had with the coach and the way the team had looked at me, betrayal in their eyes. "I'm not sure it's something I can come back from, at least not with this coach and these players."

"What did you do, Harry?" she asked, desperation in her voice. I know it must have been killing her not knowing, and perhaps it wasn't fair of me to keep this from her, but it was something out of my control.

"I'm sorry Jeri, but I can't tell you. Believe me, I would if I could, and I know this isn't going to make it any easier. I know it's hard for you and I wish things could be different, but they aren't. You just have to take my word for it."

"But did you... did you do something wrong? You should hear the things that people are saying about you."

"I can imagine," I said, frowning as I gazed up at the leafy trees standing by the side of the path. The gentle day was serene in its appearance and if it wasn't for the turmoil in my life, I think I would have found it quite relaxing. I had seen how athletic scandals played out and how people always saw them as rife for gossip. "Just don't believe anything you hear. Anyone who says anything doesn't know what they're talking about."

"But can't you tell me anything?" she asked, her voice terse. I paused for a moment, feeling like I owed her something after the way I had treated her and all that she had done for me. Jeri had always been by my side. I know that life had been hard for her because Mom and Dad always made me the priority, so maybe, in this way, I could make up some small part of it to her.

"All I can tell you is that I made a decision to do something and if I had to make the same decision again, even knowing the consequences, I would do it again. I didn't do anything selfish, and I didn't do anything to hurt anyone."

Jeri breathed a sigh of relief and nodded. "I guess that will have to be enough to satisfy Mom and Dad. They're not happy, you know."

"I can imagine. I'm sorry that you had to deal with them. I didn't realize they had been calling you so often."

"They've been on at the Dean as well. They want to try and appeal this. They're even thinking about suing the school. They're claiming that you're being treated unfairly."

I rolled my eyes. My parents had always championed me and supported me, but sometimes they were a little too zealous in their efforts to protect me.

"I'll talk to them and explain the situation. At the end of the day, this is my life and they have to abide by my decision," he said.

"So, you're really not going to fight this?"

"There is no fighting this."

"But what happens next?" she asked, looking disheartened.

"I don't know. I can still play hockey; I just can't play for the official team. I'll keep my skates sharp," I said with misplaced enthusiasm, for I knew it wasn't going to be the same.

"What about your prospects of getting called up by a pro team? Mom and Dad always said that college was your best shot at getting a contract."

"I know," I sighed. The same thought had been rattling around my mind for days. "But college isn't the only way to get ahead. I know I'm good enough to make it pro. I might just have to start lower down, maybe play a season in an amateur league or something to prove my talent, but I always believe that talent will rise to the top. They aren't going to stop me from making it," I grinned. Only I knew that I was speaking with false bravado, but it reassured Jeri.

"That's something at least. Oh Harry, I wish I could do more to help you."

I put my hand around her shoulder and pulled her close for half a hug. "You've done more than enough. I know I don't say this as often as I should, but you're the best sister a guy could ever ask for. I'm lucky to have you, and I don't want you to ever think otherwise. I'm sorry I've been a jerk recently. I've just had a lot on my mind."

"I understand," she said, and then, she grinned and her eyes twinkled. "I guess this means you're going to have more time to hang out now that you're not going to be practicing all the time!"

I laughed. "I guess so, although I think it will be a while before I'm ready to show my face on campus," I glanced around as I said this, noticing how even now, people still gazed in my direction. We continued walking along the path that lapped around the campus, making a conscious effort to stay away from the busy parts. We ended up near the entrance, where people mingled by the gate, and stopped for a while to sit on a bench underneath the shade of a tree.

"I'm sure we'll figure something else. If all else fails, you can come and hang out in my dorm."

"Oh yeah, I'm sure Angel will love that," I said dryly, chuckling at how she still held a lot of enmity for me, even after all these years.

"It's not so bad. I'm sure she'll get over her grudge though. It has been years."

"I don't really blame her. I was pretty mean to her."

"Yeah, but you've changed now," she said. I didn't disagree with her, at least not verbally, but there was a reason why I was single after all. I'd never been quite able to connect with people on a personal level. I had excelled at hockey, but everything else in my life didn't operate at a similar level. The fleeting romances I had, all crashed and burned when the girls realized that the reality of dating a star hockey player wasn't as great as the fantasy suggested, and the truth is that I never cared about any of them enough to fight for the relationship or change my ways. I always figured that, in the end, I would find someone who would inspire me to make that kind of effort, but then again, maybe I was just one of those guys who was never meant to be in a lasting relationship.

"I think she's still affected by what happened with Tommy," Jeri continued.

"That guy she was seeing? They were together for a while, weren't they?" I asked, although the memory was foggy. I never paid much attention to the lives of other people.

"Kind of. She really liked him for a long time, but they didn't get together until the very end of high school. Then they decided to stay together through college and do the long-distance thing. Angel was convinced that they were in love, and they were going to last, but then she found out that he was cheating on her. All he needed to do was be a little patient, but he couldn't even do that. It pretty much destroyed her. She couldn't believe that she had missed all the signs."

"He sounds like a jerk," I said.

"Yeah... she really needs a good man, someone who can take care of her. But I don't know if she's willing to find it. Guys check her out all the time and she doesn't even notice." I detected a hint of jealousy in her voice. I don't mean this in a bad way, but Jeri was a kind of plain looking girl compared to Angel, and I could imagine that she didn't get as much attention from guys. She'd never had a boyfriend, and I think this played on her mind, which also made it more difficult for her to get a boyfriend. Like in sports, confidence played a big part. It's like in hockey when you're one on one with the keeper, you lock eyes and in that moment, you get a sense if they're confident or not. The same thing is true in life, and if you sense that someone isn't confident, they don't seem as attractive.

"Maybe the same is true for you," I said. Jeri made a face, letting me know that she appreciated the comment, but it was a typical big brother thing to say.

"I wish. She doesn't know how lucky she is."

"I'm sure there's someone out there for you as well."

"Yeah, maybe, but the thing is, if Angel just moved on from Tommy, then she would be able to find someone like that," she snapped her fingers and shook her head, taking a sip of her coffee to try and soothe the aching anguish within her soul. I wish I knew what to say to make her feel better, but I wasn't very good at these kinds of things. At that moment her phone rang, and she groaned. I saw the word 'parents' on the screen of her phone. Before she could answer, I picked it up and swiped away, declining the call.

"What did you do that for?" she exclaimed, "they're going to be angry with me now. You know you should never hang up on them."

"No, you always take their calls. I don't. You need to be more assertive, Jeri, otherwise they're never going to give you any breaks. Just ignore them for the time being. They'll get the message, and I'll talk with them later to straighten everything out. You don't have to worry about a thing."

Jeri gnawed on her lower lip pensively and I could tell that she didn't quite believe me, but for the moment she needed to trust her big brother.

"So how is college going for you?" I asked, realizing that it had been some time since I had asked her about anything going on with her life. I suppose being kicked off the team at least meant that I would have more time to think about other people.

Jeri shrugged and tilted her head to the side. "It's pretty tough, I mean, it's a lot harder than high school and I guess I'm still trying to keep my head above water. I just wish things came as easily to me as they do to other people, but I keep plugging away and hopefully I'll get a good grade at the end of it."

"I'm sure you will. You were always the smart one of the family and you're going to go far. Hell, you might even be more of a success than me if I don't make it in hockey."

"Don't say that! I don't know what Mom and Dad would do if you didn't become a hockey player," she said, aghast.

"Yeah," I sighed, only just able to hide my dismay. Jeri again put herself down though. While I was out playing hockey, she was at home studying. She was bright, and there was nothing that could hold her back aside from her own doubts. I was about to tell her something along these lines when her gaze lingered to the entrance and then her face fell, as though she had seen a ghost.

"No... no he can't be here," she said, shaking her head slowly as though she was trying to deny what she saw with her very own eyes.

I turned around, twisting my neck to see what she was seeing. A car had pulled up and there was someone dragging a suitcase behind him, but people came and went from college all the time, so it didn't seem extraordinary.

"What's the matter? Who are you talking about?" I asked.

"That's him," Jeri said. "That's Tommy. I'm sorry Harry, but I have to go."

Like that she rose from the bench and was gone within moments. I furrowed my brow, looking at the lean, brooding figure of Tommy, Angel's ex. It was a brave man to toy with the emotions of a girl as attractive as Angel, and I wondered how he had ever brought himself to want more than she could offer. Not that it mattered to me though. I was a man alone, without even a hockey team to back me up. I finished my coffee and sighed, then retreated to my dorm to escape the stares of all those around me and their imaginings of what I had done.

Chapter Six

Angel

A gentle breeze wafted in through my window as I hunched over the desk and tried to focus on my homework. I had soft music playing in the background, but I could still hear the cries of people who were playing outside. Sometimes I wondered whether anyone actually studied around campus. Too many people treated it like a party, as Tommy had done. Apparently, he'd spent all of his time seducing other college girls instead of remembering to be my boyfriend. I wondered how easy it had been to cheat on me, and whether that said more about me or him.

My mind was wandering again, and I had to focus. I couldn't let things slip now. I had worked hard to get my average back up to something acceptable after the ordeal with Tommy had wrecked things, and I wasn't going to let the same thing happen again. At least, I had said my piece and spoken to Harry. He could do what he liked now. Hopefully, he would sort things out with Jeri, but if he didn't, there wasn't anything else I could do. She was with him now, and I hoped she would return in a good mood, otherwise I wasn't sure how to cheer her up. Perhaps I could try and set her up with a guy, although she never seemed too interested in them, and at the moment, all they'd probably want to talk about was Harry.

Maybe we were better off with some ice cream and a movie. Those things never let us down.

Jeri returned in a flurry of movement. I looked up and smiled, setting my pen down on the desk.

"How did it go? Please tell me that he actually thanked you for what you've been doing? You keep telling me that he's not a jerk to you, but so far, all I can see is someone who doesn't appreciate you."

"He did," Jeri said, panting as she tried to catch her breath. Her cheeks were flushed and strands of hair had broken away from her ponytail and were matted to her scalp, upon which beads of sweat trickled. I wasn't sure why she had bothered to run back home. "Things are fine. Thank you for speaking to him," she said, her words punctuated by deep breaths. "But there's something else you need to know. He's here," she said, leaning against the wall.

"Harry?" I asked, peering over her shoulder. Maybe he had an apology for me as well, although such a thing had been so long coming that I didn't think it would make much of a difference. It was clear to me that he didn't feel that guilty about the way he'd treated me as a kid, because he hadn't come by to apologize to me yet, and he'd had plenty of years to do so.

"No, not Harry. Tommy."

The word lanced through me like a spear. I doubled over and a sick feeling curdled inside me. My skin became hot all over and the world seemed to melt away. I didn't believe what I was hearing at first. Tommy? Here? No... no it couldn't be.

"What?" I asked, my voice hollow and terse, hoping against hope that Jeri wasn't telling the truth. She had to be mistaken. Hell, I would have taken her playing some kind of morbid trick on me over him actually being here.

But she nodded. "I saw him at the entrance, bringing his luggage in. It looks like he's moving in," she said.

My throat ran dry, and all the color drained from my face.

"No... no," I gasped, and immediately rose, sprinting out of the room. Jeri groaned and fell in step with me. We thundered out of the dorm, and she pointed to the building he had headed towards, another dorm that was likely to be his home. I couldn't believe that he had come here. I thought I was rid of him. I thought I had lanced him from my life like an ugly boil, but still, he tormented me. My face was twisted in fury as we entered the building, storming past anyone who dared get in our way. Jeri was breathless, but even so, she kept asking me whether this was really a good idea. Maybe it wasn't, but I needed to know why he was here.

When we reached the dorm, I asked around to be guided in the same direction as the new guy. I was pointed up the stairs and followed this trail until I came to a room where the door was wide open, and there he was, as though plucked from my darkest dreams, unpacking his clothes and all he had for me was a simple smile.

"Hey Angel, I was wondering when I'd bump into you," he said.

*

Time froze, as did my blood. I thought I might explode with frustration. Here he was, the man who had betrayed me, the man who had shattered my heart and destroyed my faith in love. There was his smooth, charming face with his lazy smile and dark eyes. His mane was slicked back, his slender body lithe and elegant in a strangely alluring way. This was the boy who had captured my attention when we were teenagers, who had been the star of so many fantasies on nights when I couldn't sleep, and daydreams when my mind wandered off in class. He was the standard by which I judged all other men, and they all fell short. The day when we kissed had been the happiest of my life. It felt as though all my dreams had come true and the road ahead of me was paved with gold and shone as brightly as the stars. I thought all we needed was patience. I had been ready to give all of myself to him, but that hadn't been good enough.

He had shunned the affection and devotion I had given to him.

"'Hey Angel,' that's all you have to say to me?" I said tersely, my words biting the air.

"What else is there to say? It's good to see you again, you're looking well."

I hated how casual he was, how easily he took everything in his stride as though there was no difficulty at all. I almost screamed in his face, but I managed to quell the urge.

"What are you doing here, Tommy?" I asked, each word coming out tersely, as though it had to be forced out.

Tommy shrugged and continued unpacking. "I had to transfer. Turns out my grades were suffering a little bit at my old college, and they thought it better if I seeked my education elsewhere."

"And you had to come here?"

"There really was only one choice Angel. Especially since I knew you were here." He turned and walked across the room, approaching. He seemed to glide, such was his speed. One moment he was across the room, and then he was in front of me, and I was filled with the familiar scent of him that had always played so much havoc with my mind. Before I knew it, he had taken my hand and held it so casually in his, as though it had always been and would always be meant to be held by him. He gazed into my eyes. There were so many times when I had lost myself in him, when those eyes had been an infinity to me, and I had even seen my future in them. Even now, the feeling was so powerful. This attraction I had for him had been in me for as long as I had become aware of these adult and mature feelings. They were as much a part of me as my bones, and I couldn't shake them away simply because I had been hurt.

I had to force myself to remember that he had gazed into the eyes of other girls and promised them exactly the same things he had promised me. They were all lies, slipping out of his mouth as easily as his breath.

"I thought if I came here, we might have the chance to rebuild what we lost. It was harder than I thought to maintain something over a long distance. I missed you so much and I didn't know how to handle it, but now that I've had time to reflect, I know things can be different if we just give each other a second chance. We have this opportunity now, and I've grown. I've changed. I'm not the same man who made those mistakes, Angel. After all we've been through, don't you think that we owe it to each other to give this a chance to work?"

There was a pleading, imploring tone to his voice that wormed its way into my heart. I don't know how he always could do this to me, how he could twist my thoughts and emotions into making me feel as though I was the guilty party. I took a deep breath and remembered everything that I had been through.

"You're acting as though this is something that you had no control over, like it's something that was inevitable. Just because we were in different colleges, didn't mean you had to go and cheat on me with other girls. That was a choice you made, and you have to live with the consequences."

"And I have," he stressed, he had yet to let go of my hand. "Believe me, these thoughts have weighed heavily on me every moment that we have been apart. I know that I made the biggest mistake of my life and all I ask is for the chance to make it up to you. Doesn't the fact that I'm here show that I'm willing to make the effort? I could have gone anywhere in the country, Angel, but I came here to be with you because I can't stop thinking about you. I love-"

Before he could finish the sentence, I lifted my palm away from him with a look of shock on my face. "Don't you say it," I said, pointing at him in a warning manner. He pressed his lips together and stopped mid-sentence, but he did not take back his words. I sighed. There was a time not too very long ago when I would have melted had Tommy turned up like this and said all of these things, but it was just too late. I knew what he was like now. I had peered beyond the façade and seen his true face. He had always been a liar, a thief, and if I gave into him now, he would only abuse my trust as he had done once before, and now I had to be strong. I had to deny the fleeting pangs of loneliness in my heart, the small voice that whispered to give him another chance.

"This can't happen. You can't be here. Why did you come here? Why couldn't you just leave me alone?" I asked in a plaintive voice.

"Because you are my destiny, Angel. I see that now. Whatever happened before is a mere blip in the road! It doesn't matter in the grand scheme of things. We can still do all the things you wanted. Do you remember that night you told me that you dreamed of us growing old together and thinking back on the time we spent together in our youth? We can still have that, and when we look back, we won't think of all the bad things, we'll think of how our love endured the hardships. It will be everything you want it to be."

"No," I forced myself to say. "It's not going to happen like that. If you had any respect for me, you would have stayed far away to give me space. You should have known what this would have done to me. You can't just come back here and expect me to take you back as though nothing happened. You cheated on me. You hurt me."

"And I will make all of that up to you," he said quickly, and I knew then that he didn't understand how deeply he had wounded me, how the scars on my heart would never heal.

"It's too late," I said. "I'm seeing someone else." The lie slipped out before I even knew what I was saying. All I knew is that I wanted to catch him off guard for a change. I wanted to see a look of surprise on his face and make him believe that I had fully moved on from him. For a moment, his eyes glazed over, but his smile didn't fade.

"You are?"

"Yes, I am, and I'm very happy," I said, burying myself deeper in the lie.

He withdrew his hand. "Then I look forward to meeting him, but I still don't think our story is over, Angel." He turned away from me then, ready for me to leave. My cheeks glowed red as I turned to leave the room, hating that he could reduce me to such an emotional wreck. I burst out of the doors to the dorm room, threw back my head, and screamed until my throat was raw. I didn't care who thought I was crazy, I just needed to let it all out.

"Are you quite done?" Jeri asked in a soft voice.

"Yes," I spat, glowering as I marched back to our room.

"I can't believe he's actually here. Do you think he meant all he said about wanting to get back with you?"

"I'm sure he does, and then he'll break my heart again."

"Well good on you for not believing him. I wish I had your strength. I think if someone said they wanted me this much, I would be putty in their hands," Jeri sighed.

"Yeah, well, you don't know what it's like to be treated like that," I said, and almost regretted my words. Sometimes I forget myself and remembered that Jeri was sensitive about never having had a boyfriend. I'd been thrown off my equilibrium by Tommy's appearance though, so taking care of other people's feelings wasn't exactly high on my list of priorities.

There was a moment of awkwardness as Jeri was wounded by my comment. My cheeks were flushed, and I knew I should apologize to her, but my hackles had risen, and I didn't have it in me to be kind. Blood raged around my head, and it felt like my insides were on fire.

"Why did you tell him you had a boyfriend?" she asked calmly.

"I don't know," I spat. "I just wanted to say anything that might hurt him the way he hurt me."

"You know he's going to find out the truth."

"I know," I said, again probably more harshly than Jeri deserved, but this was the effect Tommy had on me. "But I don't care right now. I can't let him get to me like this. I can't let him ruin my life again."

Chapter Seven

Angel

"You can't stay in here the whole time," Jeri said as she returned from class. I was sitting at my desk, staring at the books in front of me, trying to study. Nothing was going in. The words were a blur. In my mind, they all whizzed past me and orbited around Tommy's stupid head, which was as large as a planet. I couldn't shake the image of him mocking me with his smug charm, acting as though I should be grateful that he came here, pretending that he actually had another chance to be with me.

"I can and I will. I've worked up enough credit with my professors to do some studying from home, and I've even worked out a path where I can get to my classes without interacting with anyone if I need to," I said without looking up. Jeri chucked her bag on the floor and then perched on the edge of her bed, leaning forward and clasping her arms in between her legs.

"You know this isn't healthy Angel. You can't let him get to you like this."

I paused and closed my eyes, pressing my lips firmly together. I looked up at the ceiling and turned around slowly, leaning against the back of my chair. In my hand, I held a pen and I twisted it as a way to alleviate my stress. I wasn't sure it was working.

"I'm not letting him get to me. I'm just taking some time out to spend by myself. People do it all the time. There's nothing strange about it. I'm not becoming a recluse or anything. I just don't want anything to do with other people right now," I said.

Jeri arched her eyebrows and gave me a patronizing look. "You're shutting yourself in here because you don't want to risk running into him again," she said.

I sighed and let my hard anger fade away for a moment or two. "I know you're just worried, but can you blame me? You know how hard it was for me to get over him. Now he's back and I feel like I'm at square one again."

"Is it really that bad? I mean, you're not going to fall in love with him again, are you?" Jeri asked.

I blanched at the thought and shot her a look. "Never," I vowed. "But when I look at him, I remember the way he made me feel and how excited I was to be with him. Even though it ended badly, I still remember the good times we had, and part of me still wonders what things would have been like if we had gone to the same college in the first place."

"I don't think that would have changed who he is Angel. He still would have found a way to hurt you."

"I know, but it doesn't stop me from thinking about it. And it also makes me think about the person I was when I was with him. I think about how I was caught up in the whirling romance and how everything made sense to me. It was just... I felt good being with him, but after what he did, I don't know that I can trust anyone again."

"You will. You just need to meet the right guy."

I scoffed and tossed my hair away from my face. "And who is that going to be?"

"Angel, you do realize that half the campus would date you given a chance, right? Every time we go out, there are guys staring at you as though they've died and gone to heaven. All you need to do is give them a chance."

I sighed, noticing the envy in her voice. To be honest, I suppose a part of me had noticed it, but I had closed myself off to all those possibilities. "I haven't let myself think like that. There have been a couple of times when I have. I've thought to myself that maybe I should give this guy a try, but then I think about what happened and I this knot tightens in my chest. I can't help but think that they're going to hurt me again, or they're going to lie to me and cheat on me. I didn't see the warning signs before and I'm worried that I'm not going to be able to see them again. I just don't want to go through all that again, Jeri. I can't. I can't take it. It broke me, and it almost made me flunk out of college. I don't want that to happen, not at this stage. I'm not going to let anything get the best of me."

Jeri looked at me with sympathy and lowered her voice to a gentler tone. "Okay, I get that, Angel, I really do. I'm sure that if I was in your position, I'd probably be guarded as well. But surely you see that by staying in here, you are letting him get the better of you? I bet you haven't even been able to concentrate on work this whole time you've been here," I winced as the comment struck at my heart. Jeri always knew me better than anyone and there wasn't much that I could put past her. "I know it's hard, but it's only going to get worse if you don't face your fears. What do you think Tommy is going to think when he realizes that you're hiding yourself away? You need to show him that you're not afraid of him, that he doesn't matter to you. You need to show him that you're the boss."

I let out a dry chuckle and the smile I wore on my face was a humorless one. "And how am I supposed to do that? Every time I see him, I think I'm about to crumble. How can I possibly go through college making him believe that he doesn't mean anything to me?"

"Well, you started off by telling a lie. Maybe you should get boyfriend?"

"Didn't you just hear what I was saying?"

"I don't mean a real one, I mean get someone to pretend to be your boyfriend. If they're in on the lie, then you don't have to worry about them hurting you because it's not going to be real. You can just pretend long enough to get under Tommy's skin. Once he realizes you're not going to give him another chance he's going to move on. Come on, I think he has better things to do than to be obsessed with you for the rest of the year. When it's over you can 'break up' with this guy and carry on as normal. You won't have had to compromise yourself; you'll have dealt with Tommy, all without risking your heart."

The prospect was tempting, and she spoke in a persuasive manner. I licked my lips thoughtfully as I considered the idea, but there still was one problem.

"Even if I did go through with this, I'd have to find someone who was willing to play the role of my boyfriend. What guy is going to want to date a girl he can't actually do any of the fun things with?"

Jeri shrugged. "That's the part you're going to have to figure out by yourself. I'm only the ideas girl."

I laughed a little and considered the matter. It certainly wasn't the worst idea in the world, and if it would get Tommy off my back then maybe it had potential.

"But you know you can't go around staying in here for the rest of the year," Jeri continued. "It's bad enough that Harry is shutting himself away. I don't need two of you."

I winced at the mention of Harry and scowled at her. "I'm not like him," I spat. Jeri wore a knowing smile, but she didn't say what was on her mind and I was glad for it. I didn't want to ever think that I was like him.

*

Jeri and I talked about the matter for a while longer and, eventually, I decided that I should at least try to find someone to go along with this farce. I knew she was right that I couldn't just shut myself away. Aside from not wanting to be like Harry, it was already getting tiresome staying away from class and hiding myself in my room when I could hear everyone else having fun outside. There were some college parties coming up as well that I didn't want to risk missing out on. Tommy wasn't going to stop me from having fun at college.

Having said that, the moment I stepped out of my dorm I was instantly wary. My gaze darted about in case he was around, and my ears strained to hear him. My throat ran dry as I peered across the Met, wary of seeing him, ready to dive and duck for cover in case he should come into view. I hated that he still had this much of an effect on me. I wanted to be stronger. I wanted to be able to live my life normally without having to be married to this constant anxiety, but despite everything that happened, he was the first guy I had ever loved. I wasn't going to forget that, for better or worse. Nor was I going to forget the way he made me feel. Jeri might well be envious of me for attracting the attention of guys around campus, but there was still a nagging doubt in my mind whether I was good enough. That's what happens when someone cheats on you. All I can think about is that I wasn't enough for Tommy. I wasn't pretty enough, I wasn't fun enough, so what made people think I would be good enough for anyone else?

I took a deep breath and tried to push those thoughts away because they weren't going to do me any good here. I strode across campus, holding my head high just in case Tommy appeared from nowhere, as he had a nasty habit of doing. Thankfully I didn't bump into him on my way to another dorm, and I breathed a sigh of relief as I reached Phil's room.

Phil was a nice guy. He was always happy to help me study and I knew he had a soft spot for me. I considered him a friend and thought that he might be willing to help me out. I hadn't really connected with too many people on a personal level because of what happened with Tommy.

Phil turned around and greeted me with a smile when I knocked on his open door. I'd always found his friendly face reassuring. His eyes were kind, unlike some other people I could mention, and he had a soft manner about him. I'd never heard of any controversy surrounding him and he had never made any waves through college. Perhaps it wouldn't be so bad to have him as a fake boyfriend. If I was in a better state of mind, he might have even made a decent real boyfriend, but just the thought of getting into a relationship sent a pang through my heart.

I forced a smile and walked into the room. It was a neat and tidy room, with movie posters on the wall and books open on the desk.

"Did you finally accept my invitation to study?" he asked.

I allowed myself a small chuckle but shook my head. "Not right now. I've studied so much I think my brain is going to explode. No... I was thinking about something else actually. I have another kind of proposition for you."

"Oh?" Phil asked, tilting his head to display his intrigue.

Now that I was here, I felt stupid. My throat tightened and it was difficult for me to get the words out. I couldn't quite believe that I was about to ask him what I was about to ask him, so I sighed and just spoke quickly, as though I was ripping a band aid off an aching wound.

"I was just thinking that you're a really cool guy and you've always been nice to me," I said, and noticed the way he stood a little taller and puffed his chest out. It always seemed easy enough to inflate a man's ego. "And I wondered if you could do me a little favor?"

"I think I could manage that, what kind of favor are we talking about?" he asked.

"Well, okay, this might sound a little weird at first, but bear with me. So, it turns out that my ex just transferred here from another college and we had a pretty bad break up. I won't get into the details here, but suffice to say that it tore me up pretty bad inside and now that he's here I just... I don't know... it's hard. He seems to think that he can win me back and I want to make it clear to him that he can't, so I wondered if you'd be willing to pose as my boyfriend for a little while, just long enough so that he knows there's no chance of us ever getting back together. I know it's a lot to ask and I know it's not a normal situation, but I'd really owe you afterwards."

As I spoke the expression on Phil's face changed completely. He went from being excited to see me to quite confused. His brow furrowed and he folded his arms across his chest.

"Are you serious?" he asked.

I nodded.

"What would even... I mean... how would it work?"

"I don't know really. I haven't thought out all the details. I guess I just figured we could go out sometimes and appear around campus and act like we're together, maybe go to a party together or something, just so that people could see that we're together."

"But these wouldn't be dates?"

"No, not really, just pretend dates."

"So, you want me to go out with you, but we wouldn't really be going out, and all so that you can make this other guy jealous? And what happens at the end of it? Do we just go our separate ways and never speak of this again?"

"I haven't thought that far ahead. I just thought it would be a good way to deal with my ex, and you've always been kind to me. I know I haven't been around as much as you'd like and that's because I've been dealing with my own problems, but I always thought we could be good friends and that maybe you'd help me out with this. Believe me, I wouldn't ask this of just anyone and like I said, I'd owe you big time afterwards."

"Oh, wow, so I should feel really honored then," he grunted, shaking his head. "Look Angel, I appreciate that this probably makes sense to you, but this really isn't an ordinary situation. I mean, you do understand that, right?"

"I know," I sighed, "I just... this thing is such a mess, and I don't know how else to deal with it."

"Did you ever think of going out with a guy for real? Maybe you need a real relationship more than a fake one." He let out a humorless chuckle. "Angel, I thought I made my intentions pretty clear, but I've had a thing for you a long time now. I figured you were going through something because you always seemed distracted and stuff, but instead of messing around with all of this, how about we just go on a real date and see what happens? I think that would be better than going through all of this."

My heart skipped a beat as he asked me out for real. I hadn't been prepared for this. There was a part of me that screamed inside to say yes, but every other part was scared and worried and vulnerable. I couldn't bring myself to say yes. I froze. Every part of me went rigid and cold and this icy feeling of sickness swam in the pit of my stomach.

"Oh, Phil, that's very sweet of you, but as I said I'm not really ready for a relationship. I'd rather just go with my plan. I know it's not conventional, but I just need to get my head straight if that's alright. I know it might seem strange to you, but this is just what I need to do," I said, swallowing a lump in my throat soon after. It seemed determined to remain lodged in my throat.

"I don't think I can help you, Angel. I'm sorry. I can see that whatever you're going through has really affected you and I guess nobody should be going through that, but I don't think it's sensible for me to get involved in a situation like this. The thing is you want a fake relationship, but I'm not the type of person that can ever fake something like this. If we were going to date, then I'd want to date for real, so I think maybe you should think about that and come back to me if you change your mind and you want something better than fake."

There was a terse edge to his words. I felt ashamed and embarrassed as I left his room. I wish I was the kind of person who could have left these feelings of mistrust behind and thrown myself into another relationship. Rationally, I knew that it would be better for me in the long run, but every time I thought about getting close to someone, there was a hesitancy within me that pulled me back from the brink, as though it was stopping me from making the greatest mistake of my life. But was it a mistake, or should I have fought past this instinct to take a risk?

I suppose it doesn't matter anymore. Phil was my first choice. Is there anyone else I can have as my fake boyfriend, or would they all just react the same way Phil did?

Chapter Eight

Harry

The days were long. The nights were longer. I couldn't remember ever feeling this way before, as though my life had no purpose and no direction. I'd always had something to look forward to. Every day had always had a routine and a plan. I knew where I was going to be and what I was doing. It was so regimented it was like the army, and I wondered if soldiers felt the same way as me when they returned from active duty. The hours slipped into each other without any kind of rhythm or structure. My hands and limbs twitched, aching to get out on the ice. I spent the time trying to calculate how many hours I had spent playing hockey during my life and I stopped when I figured it must have been in the high thousands at least. It had been the biggest thing in my life and now it was just gone, and even though I would have made the same choice again if I had the chance, it didn't make it hurt any less.

I just couldn't believe the team had turned its back on me. I had given everything to hockey and I always assumed that I would get everything back in return, but now I saw how little loyalty there was. It was easy to be jaded and to give up. I didn't want to. There was still fire burning in my heart, but I didn't know where to go from here. I tried to be positive for Jeri's sake, but the fact is I didn't know whether I was going to be able to make it as a pro any longer. The natural steppingstone to the professional leagues was through college. That's where the majority of the scouts went and where I should be making a name for myself. The other option, which was looking more and more likely, was going through the amateur leagues. It wasn't the worst thing in the world, although I'd have to get a job to support myself, and I had heard horror stories about gifted players toiling in the leagues for years without ever getting picked up by pro teams. Then there was always the danger of getting on the bad end of an injury as well and losing all hope.

The odds had always been against me making it as a pro hockey player just because there were so many people vying for a limited number of positions on the roster of professional teams, but things had never seemed so bleak for me. I had always had a sense of control before. I always felt like my destiny was in my own hands because, as long as I could get on the ice, then I knew what I was doing and I could impress whoever was watching, but now... now it all seemed as though it was slipping away from me.

It didn't help that my parents were overreacting as usual. I ended up calling them back after Jeri said she was getting the brunt of their ire, so I had to brace it as they poured out all their concerns and worry onto me. My ear still burned from talking to them on the phone for so long. It took me ages to convince them to not storm down to college and challenge the decision. They weren't happy with me, but eventually they believed me when I said it wouldn't make any difference. I could see why they were worried because they had spent so much time and money in giving me the opportunity to pursue hockey, but even I was starting to believe they were getting a little over the top with it. I mean, at the end of the day, if I didn't become a hockey pro then I would still be alive. As much as I loved hockey, I didn't want to define myself by it, and sometimes, I felt as though my folks saw a hockey player before they saw a son.

But I guess that's just another thing that I'd have to deal with. It wasn't as though the situation was going to get any better.

Speaking of which, I had to get out of my room. I'd been hiding myself away ever since the incident, but I was beginning to lose my mind. Jeri coaxed me out a few times to grab a coffee, but I could feel the lingering looks and I could hear the whispers. They made the back of my neck warm with tingles, and there was an uneasy feeling inside. Part of me wanted to yell at all of them and get them to ask their questions, to get all of it out of their system, but I knew then that I'd be seen as the crazy man on campus. I knew some of the rumors that were flying around, and I knew the likely source of them. My blood boiled with anger, but what could I do?

I'd been given some leeway from my professors about missing classes, but that slack was being rescinded as more days went by. My grades weren't anything to be impressed with either. I had always done just enough to get by while focusing on hockey, but now I didn't have hockey to fall back on. My grades were all I had, and I thought that, now I had more time to study, they would improve, but it turned out I wasn't all that good at studying. Having more time didn't equate to getting better results, and it certainly didn't make me more intelligent. I started to wonder if college had been a waste of time after all.

I left for class with a heavy weight in my heart. As soon as I stepped out of the dorm, I could feel the tension in the air. Even when people didn't look at me, I knew they were thinking about me and what they thought I'd done. It was inescapable, like a fog that settled over the campus, but I was standing alone in it while everyone else was looking at me, seeing me as the enemy. I walked briskly and kept my head down, hoping to avoid as much attention as possible. It felt abnormal doing this. Usually, I felt like a celebrity walking around campus. Most people used to smile at me, and they were always happy to see me and have a little chat, usually about my performance in a recent game. I had always felt a part of things, as though I was as much a part of the college as the buildings and the teachers, that I was being woven into the history of this place. Now I realized that I wasn't anything special and once I graduated – if I graduated – nobody would think much of me.

I almost reached class when I heard them come up behind me. I had turned into a small path between two buildings in a part of the campus that was usually deserted. I realized they must have been following me. I sighed as I halted, turning around, because I'd never been the kind of man to run from his problems.

"What do you guys want?" I asked.

There were three of them. Chase was flanked by Bobby and Timo. Chase had long hair that he always pulled away from his face like curtains. Bobby was stocky and wide, his face ruddy and fleshy, with hair shaved to the scalp. Timo was a giant Finnish exchange student with a face like granite. I had only ever seen him wear one expression, and the only variation was in how mean he looked.

"We just wanted to say hi, to make sure that you're doing okay. It's been a while since we've seen you around," Chase said, the words slipping out of his mouth like quicksilver. His lips twitched into a smirk and there was a darkness in his eyes. On the ice, it had manifested itself in sly play. Chase's quick hands were talented, but I had recently realized that there was something even darker behind them, and his deviousness was a part of him on and off the ice.

"I've been keeping quiet, you know, keeping to myself. I figured we'd all be doing that," I said.

"Well, yes, it's been quite a trying time for the team. I just want to make sure that things aren't going to change. We all know the damage you could cause," Chase said.

I grimaced and spoke through gritted teeth. "We've already been over this Chase. I know what was agreed. Let's just leave it. I don't want anything to do with you."

"But we're not done with you yet. There's still a little payback we need to have," he said. Bobby and Timo moved more quickly than I could react. I lifted a hand to try and defend myself against Bobby, but he had already swiveled behind me and grappled me, using his history in wrestling to good use. Timo snarled and drove a fist into my stomach as hard as a battering ram. All the wind was knocked out of me, and I was only standing because Bobby held me up. Another blow came, this one right across my face. Pain bloomed and I could taste the warm flow of blood in my mouth. This time, Bobby did let go and I dropped to the ground like a stone. I gasped for breath, but wasn't given a chance to catch it as Chase came in and kicked me. It was just like him to get the final blow without doing any of the hard work. Pain flared across my chest. I turned to look up at them, three of them towering above me, wondering if they were going to put me out of my misery.

"This is just a final warning Harry. Don't ever think about telling anyone the truth of what happened, otherwise there will be consequences. We'll be seeing you around," Chase said. He went to kick me again and I flinched, eager to get my body out of the way, but he stopped just short of kicking me and laughed with glee at how he had rendered me so scared. I scrunched my face up in anger and wished that I could have had him all to myself. Then we'd see how much he'd laugh.

Once they were gone, I dusted myself off and pulled myself up, wiping the blood from my lips. I winced in pain and limped away, feeling more alone than I had ever been before. All through my life, I never had to worry about being alone because I had always had a team backing me up. But now that team had turned its back on me and when I looked around everyone viewed me with suspicion. Even now as I limped through campus nobody came to help me. Hell, they probably thought I deserved whatever I have been given. They all had their own ideas of what I'd done. Nobody knew the truth. Nobody could ever know the truth.

Chapter Nine

Angel

The last few days had been hell. I felt like an idiot for going to Phil with this. Jeri didn't seem all that surprised that he had turned me down. For someone who had never had a boyfriend before she seemed to have a pretty good idea of how men's minds worked.

"I guess you can see why he wouldn't do it. I don't think I'd want to go out with someone if I knew nothing was going to come of it, especially if I liked them," she said.

"Well, I'm glad you told me this before I made a fool of myself. This was your idea in the first place," I said, a little aggrieved that she seemed to be abandoning the benefits of her idea too late for me not to make a fool of myself.

"I think it might be one of those ideas that sound better in theory than in practice. It depends on the kind of guy you find really, but most people are going to want to date you for real, Angel. Even if you did find someone who agreed to date you, would you be willing to bet that they wouldn't develop feelings for you? You're just that kind of girl, people gravitate towards you. I wish I knew your secret."

"There is no secret," I said dryly. "Jeri, we both know you're great and, if guys don't see that, it's their problem, not yours. You've always had a better head on your shoulders than I have and I'm sure you're going to find someone who loves you before too long."

"Yeah, and how long have you been saying that for? Do you remember in high school when nobody asked me to prom? You told me not to worry because high school guys just didn't know how to appreciate someone like me, and that I should wait until college because then I'm going to have all of them flocking to me because they'd be more mature. Well now we're in college and still nothing is happening. Are you going to tell me that I need to wait until we're out in the real world? I'm tired of waiting Angel," she said, her voice terse, her pale features crimson. Usually, Jeri was the calm one, the one who had everything under control and maintained her equilibrium, but recently I noticed that she was teetering a little more. I had been so concerned with my own problems that I perhaps hadn't given her the time she needed as a friend.

"What's wrong Jeri?" I asked.

At first, she looked angry, probably wondering why I even needed to ask when it was so obvious, but she softened quickly and slumped to the bed. She held her hands in her lap and looked utterly defeated.

"I just don't know what I'm doing. I never thought my life would be like this, you know? I've always been the forgotten one. I've been in Harry's shadow, and I've been in yours as well."

"That's not true," I protested, but I was silenced with a look.

"You don't have to try and reassure me Angel. I know what it's been like. Harry was the star hockey player, and I was the dutiful sister who behaved well and didn't cause any trouble. You're the pretty one and I'm the friend that stands by your side no matter what. I always just figured that, at some point, it would be my turn to stand in the spotlight... but the longer it takes, the more it feels like it's never going to happen, and I can't help but think that whatever I'm doing so far isn't working."

"You don't have to be so upset about it, Jeri. Life isn't a race. There's no deadline that you have to meet or anything. You'll meet the right guy, I know you will."

Jeri didn't look convinced at all. "I'm not sure there is a 'right' guy. It's just that you and Harry have both had your dramas and I feel like I'm the one who isn't allowed a meltdown, because I have to be there for you both, and I'm just tired of it. I want to feel like I'm allowed to freak out, that I'm allowed to be someone else. Sometimes I feel like I should just give it all up, go get drunk at a party and just jump on the first guy who is willing. I just want to get it over with, Angel. I can't take it anymore. You don't know what it's like inside, this ache, this feeling that I'm never going to know what it's like to be with anyone."

"Jeri, come on, you know you don't want that, not really. I know it's hard, but you will meet a good guy. There's one out there for you, I promise," I said, knowing that the words rang hollow. I wish I knew the right things to say, but I couldn't conjure a boyfriend out of the air for her. I hated how she was so upset by this. I wish I could have made her feel better, but it was beyond my power.

"I'm not sure what I want anymore," she said. "I need to go for a walk."

I called after her, but she insisted that she wanted to be alone, so I let her go. I turned back to my desk and wondered if I had been too selfish about things. Had I been so consumed with my own problems that I had stopped being a good friend to Jeri? I vowed that I would redouble my efforts as there was nobody more important to me. I guess she had been pretty overwhelmed with me and Harry, stupid Harry letting her worry about him so much. He could be so selfish sometimes. I might have to have another word with him.

It felt as though everything was crumbling around me. I had worked so hard to build a solid foundation to my life. Jeri was one of the pillars that held everything up after Tommy had ruined everything, and if she wavered then I wavered too. Tommy's return had cast everything in doubt, and I wondered if life was just a case of lurching from one disaster to the next. Were things ever going to get better?

*

There was a soft knock at the door and at first, I wondered if Jeri had returned and felt guilty about her outburst, but this was her room as much as it was mine so there was no reason for her knock. My second guess was that it was one of the guys I had asked to be my fake boyfriend. Perhaps they had reconsidered, although none of them seemed enthused with the idea. It turned out that guys didn't really appreciate the idea of having a fake relationship without getting any of the good parts. I also realized, through my efforts to find a fake boyfriend, that I didn't know as many people as I thought I did, at least not on a personal level. There were faces that I recognized across campus and names that drifted through my mind, but they were just people who populated my world, ones that I had never allowed myself to get close to. I had spent so much time wrapped up in my relationship with Tommy that I hadn't spent enough time becoming involved in the social scene at college, and thus I was a stranger in their midst.

My third guess was that it was Tommy, and this fear was so powerful that I almost stopped myself from opening the door at all. I was all alone, and it wouldn't have been difficult for him to find out where my dorm was. What if he had found out that I was lying about having a boyfriend? I could just imagine him coming in, all smug and arrogant, making me feel stupid, telling me that I must still like him, otherwise I wouldn't have made up such a dramatic lie. He'd twist my feelings and taunt me and try to turn me inside and out. I couldn't let him. I wouldn't let him. I also wasn't going to give him the power to ruin my entire life. There was another knock on the door, this time more insistent. I pressed my lips firmly together and resisted the urge to hide away from the world for one moment.

To my surprise it was Harry standing there, and he looked the worse for wear. He was doubled over. There was a dark shadow of a bruise across his face. His lip was cracked, and he groaned whenever he moved. As much as I disliked him, I didn't want to see him like this.

"Is Jeri here?" he asked, his voice weak and pained.

"No, she's gone out," I replied. Harry nodded and turned away.

"Wait, come in. You look like you could use some help," I said. Harry came in and sat on Jeri's bed. I fetched him some cotton wool balls drenched in cold water, and he held them to his face, wincing as he did so. He lifted his shirt and I almost retched as I saw an ugly bruise spreading across his stomach, as though someone had spilled ink over him. I also couldn't help but notice the hard angles of his muscles and the bed of hair that spread over the expanse of his torso. There was something so masculine about him and it made an instinctive part of me twitch, and I hated myself for it.

"That looks painful. You should go to the nurse for that," I said.

Harry shook his head vehemently. "I'm not going there. If I go there, they'll only ask what happened. It's not worth the trouble. It'll heal. I've had worse before," he said. I couldn't understand how anyone could get used to that much pain. I'd seen him be battered and clattered on the ice before, and I wondered if it was the same as getting a heart shattered.

"It looks pretty bad. Are you sure you shouldn't go to the nurse or the hospital?"

"No," he said bluntly. It was clear that he hadn't lost any of his natural charm.

"Why not? What would you have to tell them?" I asked.

"I should come back when Jeri's here. She used to patch me up whenever I needed it," Harry said, ignoring the question. He went to rise, but the pain was too much, and he settled back on the bed immediately. I got him some water, figuring it was the polite thing to do, and I was thinking of Jeri as well. I knew the animosity between Harry and myself was hard for her to deal with and since she was going through a hard time, I wanted to make things easier for her.

He thanked me for the drink and took a sip.

"So, what happened then? Is this some weird hazing ritual that goes on? Are you trying to fight your way back onto the team?"

He shook his head. "No, it was just a misunderstanding, that's all."

"Some misunderstanding," I said dryly, shaking my head. I don't know why guys had to be so secretive all the time, but it never seemed to do them any good. "I guess you're still not being forthcoming about what happened then. Have you even told Jeri?"

He wore a scowl, giving me all the information I needed.

"I haven't told anyone."

"Why not?"

"Because it's a matter for the hockey team and the hockey team alone."

"Oh, I see, because the hockey team is its own little world."

"Something like that," he said, taking another sip of his drink.

I shook my head and laughed. He made the whole thing sound more dramatic than what it needed to be. It was clear that something else was going on though, if he was being beaten up like this. I couldn't help but wonder what he had done that would cause people to treat him like this. Jeri was still staunchly defending him, but I thought that the truth might have come out by now. Everyone was being tight lipped about it, so what had actually happened? I hated not knowing things. Secrets only ever caused trouble, but I suppose it was par for the course that Harry should be causing trouble.

"Well, you might want to stay away from Jeri for a while until that fades. I think it's a good thing that she's not around at the moment. She's not in the best place right now."

"I know this has been hard on her," he said, and I actually saw guilt in his face. I wasn't sure he was capable of the emotion. "I never meant to get her involved like this. She's the only one I have though. She's the only one who believes in me."

"Maybe that would change if you told people the truth," I said. He remained silent.

"What do you mean she's not in the best place?"

"We just had a talk about things. I think she's finding it hard. She's pretty lonely. I think she just wants a boyfriend really."

"Oh, yeah, I guess it might have been brought on by the fact your ex is back," he said. I felt as though cold water had been poured over me. It made sense that Jeri would talk about it with Harry, but to hear him speak about it so nonchalantly made my skin crawl. It was supposed to be my business, not his. After the way he had treated me, he didn't get to speak about my life like this.

"What do you know about that?" I asked, my voice brittle and sharp. Harry didn't seem to detect any extra edge to it, or if he did, he didn't care.

"Just what Jeri said, that you guys had a bad break up and now he's transferred here."

I breathed a sigh of relief. At least Jeri hadn't told Harry about my plan to get a fake boyfriend.

"Yes, well, I think the whole thing is getting to Jeri a little bit. She has this idea that guys are ready and willing to throw themselves at me and I'm being ungrateful by not taking up the opportunity to date them."

"She's always had something of an inferiority complex. I suppose I can't blame her. I'm as much at fault as anyone, but our parents didn't really take the time to encourage her as much as they did me. I think I was aware of it as a kid, but I didn't know that anything was that wrong. I guess I figured that, because Mom and Dad thought it was alright, it must have been alright. It's stupid really because Jeri has always been so much better than me at everything else. I mean, at the end of the day all I do is hit a puck with a stick. She's the one who gets good grades and knows how to keep a place clean. She's the one who has it all together. I hate that she can't seem to see it."

"I know," I said softly, amazed that Harry and I were actually agreeing on something. "She's always lacked confidence though. If she would put herself out there a little bit more, I think she would do better. I'm sure plenty of guys would like a girl like her, they just need to get to know her a bit more. I'm surprised that you never set her up with anyone on the team."

Harry recoiled back, acting as though I had said something truly shocking. "I would never do that. None of them are good enough for her. Besides, I wouldn't want her to be with a hockey player. It's not a good way to live."

"What do you mean?"

He sighed softly, embracing some of the pain inside him, pain that I didn't know he had. "It's just hard. It takes up a lot of time, especially if you want to be the best. What with all the practice and all the training and then there are the matches, and if you want to be strict then you need to have a good schedule as well, and a diet, and that means no alcohol either."

"You don't drink?" I asked, my eyes widening in shock. I thought every college student got drunk now and then just as a matter of course, but Harry shook his head.

"I've had a taste here and there, but it wouldn't help me play hockey, so I never drank that much. Never partied much either. I pretty much never stay up past eleven, so as you can imagine I haven't enjoyed the full experience of college and a routine like that doesn't leave much room for romance."

I suppose I had never considered that Harry hadn't had many girlfriends. There had always been girls with crushes on him because of his status as the star hockey player, and I just assumed that those would have transformed into relationship, but now that I thought about it, I suppose I hadn't heard Jeri speak about his girlfriends. This was the first time Harry and I had had a proper conversation for years, and it reminded me how little I knew about him. I figured that he would have spent his time enjoying everything that college had to offer. I didn't think about the toll it would have taken on his life. I may not have liked him, but I had to admire the dedication to his sport. It must have hurt him that it was all over now.

"I suppose you have the chance to catch up on all that now though," I said, wondering if there was too much spite in my voice.

"Yeah, I guess I do," he said. He gazed into space, as though he was peering beyond the veil of the world. I surprised myself for feeling sympathy for him in that moment. It was clear he was struggling with things. Hockey had been everything to him. When everything was taken away what did he have left?

We descended into silence. I wasn't sure what to say again, and neither was he. The only common ground we had was Jeri, despite knowing each other all our lives. But this was the first time that we were together where I didn't just see him as the guy who had bullied me for so many years. I had let that image define the idea of him I had in my mind for so long, but he had grown and so had I. It didn't change the fact that it had happened or the way I felt about him, but it did at least show that we had both grown and changed. Since neither of us were sure what to say to each other, Harry took his leave shortly after this and I was left to ponder on what had happened with him. I didn't understand why anyone would have beaten him like that, or how he could put up with it and not tell anyone. There was definitely something bigger going on here, and I hated how it was being hidden behind this secretive veil, as though the hockey world was sacred, and nobody should ever get a peek in.

*

It was about an hour later when Jeri returned. She looked sheepish and apologized for her outburst earlier.

"It's okay," I reassured her. "Everyone is allowed to let things get the better of them now and then. I think we both know that I've done it more than once," I said.

She smiled, but I could tell she still felt strange about it. "I just wish that I knew how to make things better. I wish that I was more like you, Angel."

I laughed at this, which I didn't mean to be disrespectful, but I suppose it came across like that. "I don't know why you'd want that, Jeri. You're much better than I am."

"The world doesn't see it that way."

"You'll get there, Jeri, and I'll be with you every step of the way. You know that this isn't the way it's always going to be. You're going to fall in love and when you do it's going to be worth the wait, and I'll be right there to enjoy it with you."

Her face lit up. "Do you really think so?"

"I know so. And given the way things are at the moment, I'm almost a hundred percent sure that you're going to fall in love again before I am."

This time it was Jeri's turn to scoff with laughter and shake her head. "There's no way that's possible. You could get any guy you wanted, Angel. We both know that's true. The only thing that's getting in your way is what happened with Tommy. Look, maybe we both need to get out of our own heads a bit. I saw some fliers around campus. There's going to be a big party for the next hockey game. I thought we could go, maybe have a few drinks and loosen up a bit. They're showing it on a big screen at the Met. It should be awesome, like a drive-in movie, except without the cars."

"I thought you only watched hockey when Harry was playing?"

Jeri's cheeks turned red, as though she had been holding onto a dirty secret all these years.

"Actually, I kinda do like the game. It's hard to watch it so often without appreciating it."

Speaking of Harry, I decided not to tell Jeri about what happened with him as I didn't want to worry her. She had too much on her mind already and it wasn't fair to keep putting things on her. I think she was right when she said that Harry and I asked too much of her. We always went to her whenever we had a problem and, sometimes, I forgot that she had problems of her own. Christ, did Harry and I have something in common? The thought made my insides turn.

"I'll think about it," I said, not sure that I really wanted to be out among all those people, but Jeri had done enough for me over the years, so this was really the least I could do. And it might not have been so bad. Perhaps it would do me some good to get out, and really throw myself into college life rather than hiding deep in my room, waiting for the world to end.

Chapter Ten

Angel

Nerves fluttered in my stomach as we got ready for the party. I never used to get this nervous, but I had a feeling that something was going to go wrong during the night. I also didn't care that much for hockey. I would have pulled out if Jeri hadn't been so excited. Once we made the decision to go to the party, she had been buzzing with excitement and I didn't want to back out now, not when she had always been so supportive of me. I forced a smile and feigned excitement.

"It's just a shame Harry didn't want to come," Jeri said as she fastened earrings to her ears. She looked great actually, having made an effort to doll herself up. She had even gone shopping to get a new outfit, and Jeri hated shopping.

"Yeah, I guess it's understandable though. I can't imagine he'd want to watch his old team go and play knowing that he should be on the ice."

"I just wish he'd tell me what happened so I could try and fix it."

"Maybe that's the problem; maybe there is no fixing it," I said.

Jeri sighed and shrugged. "I just think it would be good for him to get out. I know you're going to hate me for saying this, but you two have more in common than you think."

"You're right, I do hate you for saying that. I'm nothing like him."

"You both spend too much time in your own heads," Jeri continued as though I hadn't spoken at all. "It would do you both good to get out. I suppose I'll have to do more work on Harry though. At least, he's started going to classes again. I really hope he works enough to make it out of college. He always banked on hockey and now that's gone I don't know what he's going to do if he fails."

"Didn't he ever come up with a backup plan?"

Jeri shook her head. "Mom and Dad never let him. They said that making a backup plan was only casting doubt. They said he had to move forward with complete focus and belief that he was going to make it in hockey, because that was the only way he would succeed."

"That sounds harsh. It's a lot of pressure."

"Yeah, they were always hard on him and kept pushing him. I know, sometimes, I've been jealous of him because of the attention he got, but when I look back at it now, I was at least allowed to play with my toys and hang out with my friends. Harry was just always told to practice and practice and watch tapes of him practicing when he wasn't out on the ice. He never really got to be a kid. I guess it always seemed as though it was a worthy sacrifice to be made once he made it big, but if he's not going to be a hockey player then you kind of have to ask whether it really was worth it."

"I had no idea your parents were so strict," I said, or that Harry had had it so bad.

"Yeah, well, I don't like to speak bad about them. I guess, as I'm getting older, I'm realizing that they're just people and they're capable of making mistakes, like the rest of us. I can see why they wanted to push Harry so hard, but I wish they were easier on him because now he just seems lost all the time, as though he's only going through the motions. Everything in his life revolved around hockey. All his friends were his teammates. Now he has none of that left. At least, if he came tonight, he'd have a couple of friendly faces."

"Well, one," I said.

Jeri shot me a look. "Are you really still upset with him for the way he treated you as a kid?"

The force of her question took me by surprise. "Of course, I am. It hurt. It still hurts today when I think about it."

"He only teased you a little bit. It was a long time ago."

"It doesn't feel that long ago," I said. I thought about the way I used to run home in tears because of something he had said or done, and how I used to doubt myself all the time because he acted as though everything I did was always worthy of mockery.

"I get that, I really do, but don't you think that maybe part of your problem is that you dwell on things too much?"

"What do you mean?"

Jeri sighed. "It's just something that has come up in class recently. Do you promise you're not going to get angry if I try and give you some advice?" she asked, turning towards me.

I nodded, encouraging her to continue even though I wasn't sure I was going to like what she had to say.

"It's just that, with this and with the Tommy thing, I worry that you hold onto things too much. Yeah, I get that they hurt and they're important markers in your life, but it might be a sign that you're too willing to keep these things close. I mean, it's getting to the point where they're preventing you from moving on with your life, and it's not healthy. I just think it might be an idea to take stock of these feelings and ask yourself why you're holding onto them and whether there's anything you can do that might make your outlook a little more positive."

I stared at her blankly, feeling as though she had just peeled away an old wound. My first instinct was to be sharp with her, but I told myself that she was just trying to help in her own way.

"I think I handle things just fine. We should probably head out now or we're going to miss the start of the game," I said, marching out of the room as Jeri finished fixing her hair, not giving her a chance to respond. I hated how close to the mark she was, and how she knew me better than anyone else. But I had to hold onto this pain otherwise I was at risk of making the same mistakes again.

*

The tension between us dissipated as we made our way out onto the huge field that stretched across the Met. The moon was bright and flanked with stars, although I could hardly see them since there were lamps set up all around the field, making the light bloom like flowers.

The Met was already teeming with people, clustered in groups, drinking beer and laughing merrily. I felt myself wince as I was thrust into this cacophony of happiness, feeling as though I didn't belong. Everywhere I looked, there was another smiling face and it almost seemed as though they were taunting me.

"It's going to be okay," Jeri said, gently urging me forward as though I was a child anxious to go to my first day of school. I licked my lips and told myself that it was all going to be okay. It was just a game of hockey, after all. I hated how crippled I felt though, and it was all because of Tommy. This college had been a sanctuary for me, but now that I knew he was here, it had become fraught with danger. His presence lingered like a malevolent spirit, and he could strike at any moment. I had managed to avoid him since I had sought him out, but that didn't do anything to soothe the anguish in my heart. I knew that he was still out there, waiting to torment me again.

Jeri and I moved through the field, and I looked up at the towering big screen that would show the game. I breathed deeply, telling myself to just focus on that rather than my trauma. I kept telling myself that I shouldn't let Tommy have this much power over me, but it was so hard to shake the habits I had formed. I let the bubbling murmur settle my nerves and tried to lose myself in the ambient noise. After my initial discomfort, I had to admit that there was something refreshing about being a part of the crowd. Despite the fact that the game had not started yet, cheers and chants were already beginning to erupt from various parts of the crowd. People wore huge foam hands and were dressed in the uniform of the team, ready to put their support to the players who were treated as stars.

I found that my thoughts turned to Harry, which surprised me. He must have lived for nights like this before. I heard people discussing how the team was going to perform without him and whether he should have been allowed to play despite whatever had happened, as though his prowess on the ice was enough to absolve him of any crime.

I was disgusted when I overheard some people say that they didn't care whether he had raped someone, as long as he brought the championship home, but it was worse for Jeri who had to listen to these wild accusations being thrown around about her brother. We moved away whenever we heard a comment like this, and I'm sad to say that we moved around fairly often.

And then I saw him. I froze. He was standing there, Tommy, with a group of friends he'd made who were laughing and joking, because they didn't know what kind of monster he was. They didn't know what he was capable of. He had cast his spell on them just as he cast his spell on everyone he met, and people only saw the truth when it was too late. It had been too late for me. He acted as though he didn't have any care in the world, and I hated him for how he found it so easy to adapt to life here. Already, he had a group of friends, which was more than I could say for myself. Life was so easy for him. He could glide through everything without suffering any consequences for it. My cheeks burned red as I stared daggers at him. Jeri tried to pull me away. I could hear her in the vague distance. Her voice was tinny and faint as she told me that we should leave, that it wasn't worth getting upset about, but it was already too late; he had seen me.

He sauntered over in that casual way of his, as though he had all the time in the world, as though everything would pause for him. His lazy smile was not quite a smirk and not quite a grin. His voice was quiet, and yet, powerful enough that I could hear him over everything else.

"What a pleasure it is to see you here, Angel, Jeri," he said, momentarily turning to Jeri before his gaze rested upon me. It was always for me, as though he didn't know how to leave me alone. "I had a feeling you'd be here. It's nice to be at an event where everyone shows so much passion. Please, won't you come and join me and my friends?" he asked.

"No," I said through gritted teeth. My entire body had gone so rigid that it trembled and, as much as I could tell myself that he didn't have control of me, putting that into practice was extremely difficult. There was just a part of me that went off, like a switch was flicked, whenever he was near.

"Oh, that's such a shame. I suppose you must already have plans. Perhaps you're meeting this boyfriend of yours, yes?" He craned his neck around as if to make a mockery of my lie. Did he know? He always had a way of knowing what was on my mind. I just wish that I had his instinct for sniffing out lies. I might have saved myself a whole lot of pain. "Well, he's welcome to join us of course. It would be a pleasure to meet him. I'd love to meet the man who has stolen your heart from me."

I bristled with anger. How dare he act as though my heart was his to steal.

"I need to go," I said tersely and spun on my heels, walking away from him, not caring whether he thought I was a coward or even just crazy. All I knew is that I didn't want to be around him at that moment. I waltzed away, with Jeri following, trying to pull me back. She grabbed a hold of my arm and I turned to face her with wild eyes. Emotions were all over the place.

"Angel! You can't leave. You should stay. You should face him. You're never going to get over this if you keep running away," she said in a terse, low voice, trying to make it so that Tommy couldn't overhear us, but I knew he would be watching and listening. Nothing escaped his attention.

"I don't care. I can't be around him. Just seeing him again makes my blood boil. If I stay here, I'm going to scream," I shot back.

"Please," she said in a desperate voice, a whimpering look upon her face. "I wanted this to be a good night for us. We can go somewhere else. It's a big field. We don't have to be anywhere near him. We can just ignore him."

"I can't do that, Jeri. I'm sorry. I can't be out here knowing that he's out here. I just can't. I need to leave." I walked away, hating myself for leaving Jeri like that, when I knew there was nothing she wanted more than to enjoy a relaxing night with other people watching the hockey, but my stomach churned and tears welled in my eyes. I felt everyone watching me, but most of all I knew that he was there, and I had to be anywhere else. I pushed my way through the crowd, stifling my sobs, retreating to the only safe place I knew, hoping that Jeri would be able to forgive me.

Chapter Eleven

Harry

Wherever I went I was haunted by what I had lost. I tried to put on a brave face, but I couldn't escape the fact that a hockey game was taking place, and everything was building up to it. I noticed how people shut their jaws when I came by, as though I wasn't allowed to even talk about hockey, let alone play it. It drove me crazy. I knew it would be hard, but I didn't realize it would be this hard. I had only just come to realize how much of my life hockey made up, and how empty it was when it was taken away. I had sacrificed so much for the sake of the sport, but it had not been kind to me in return. No, that wasn't quite fair. It wasn't the sport's fault; it was the people on the team.

I shuddered as I thought about what had happened and wondered how things might have been different if I hadn't seen what I did, or if I had just walked away and ignored what happened. But if I had, then I wouldn't have been able to live with myself. Sadly, there was always a price to pay for integrity, but it was still a price I had been willing to pay.

But a night like this was hard. I heard about the party on the Met of course, where everyone was gathering to watch the game. I saw people going there early to get a prime spot, setting up a barbecue. I remembered the excitement before a game, thinking about how everyone at college would be watching and cheering me on, knowing that if I played well, I would return as a hero. That wasn't my fate this time. No matter what happened on the ice, I wasn't going to be treated as anything other than a regular student. Not everyone was on the Met though. Some people stayed in their dorms and watched it together, enjoying private parties where they could drink a little more than they were allowed and smoke without campus security coming to dull their buzz. I heard the raucous chants as they got ready for the evening, and I couldn't take anymore. I left my room and went out for a walk, grabbing a bottle of whiskey as I did so.

I sipped from it as I walked across campus. I avoided the Met, but even from this vantage point I could see the towering screen and the flickering images as they prepared to show the game. Bitterness swam within that I tried to dull with the biting liquor, but I wasn't entirely successful. There was only one person I could turn to now, one person who would make this all feel better.

The dorms were deserted as I walked through the empty halls, and I was faced with closed door after closed door. But then I reached Jeri's room and the door was ajar. I heard sobbing sounds coming from inside and I peered in, worried about my sister, but it wasn't Jeri at all. It was Angel. She was spread over her desk, her blonde hair cascading along her back like a golden waterfall, and her shoulders shuddered with sorrow.

I knocked softly to announce my presence, but she didn't seem to hear. I cleared my throat and asked if she was okay. She lifted her head and turned. Her eyes were raw and watery, her cheeks flushed.

"Go away!" she screamed and swiped her hand through the air in an effort to banish me from the room, but I knew from experience that you should never let anyone cry alone, and I hadn't walked all this way to leave again.

"I would but I have nowhere else to go," I sighed as I sank on Jeri's bed, taking another deep sip of whiskey. I could already feel my head swimming. "What's going on?"

"I'm not going to tell you. You don't care. Just leave Harry. I don't want to talk about it. I want to be alone."

"Do you? I thought I wanted to be alone as well, but when you're alone, all you have are your own thoughts running around your mind and it's all so horrible. I don't think I can leave you alone for your own good, and I don't want to be alone either. But hey, we have whiskey and that makes it all better."

I thought Angel was going to scream at me again, but instead, she looked at me and dried her eyes. She pulled her hair around and smoothed it down. "I thought you didn't drink?" she asked.

I responded with a dry, bitter laugh. "I didn't drink when I played hockey. I couldn't afford to, but now that I don't have hockey, there's nothing stopping me. I'm finally free," I said, my words rolling along the rhythm of my laugh.

"I thought you were going to play for an amateur club?"

"I don't know anymore. I don't know whether I have it in me. After what happened I... I think I might need some time before I'm a part of a team again," I caught myself before I said too much. "Where's Jeri?"

"She's out watching the game. I thought she might come back with me, but I guess she wants to be out there. I can't blame her."

"Seems like everyone does. I bet you and I are the only two people not there. You were never a fan of hockey, were you?"

"Not really," she said, shrugging. "But I was happy to see the game tonight I just... couldn't."

"Why not?"

She looked away and reached across herself, stroking one shoulder. "I just couldn't. Tommy was there," she said in a small voice.

"Oh, your ex, right? I still don't get why he'd choose to come to this place after everything that happened. I couldn't imagine going to the same college as an ex. It would just make things awkward."

"I know right, but Tommy doesn't care about that. He just wants to make my life a living hell. He doesn't care about anything other than tormenting me."

"Dude sounds like he needs to get a life. What a jerk. To be honest I never liked him anyway."

"You didn't?" Angel laughed.

"Hell no, I could tell from the first time I met him that he was a jerk."

"Well thanks for telling me." She shook her head and scowled before she reached towards me, flexing her fingers to try and get me to hand over the whiskey. "If we're going to talk about him then I'm going to need some of that." I let her have the bottle. She arched her neck back and took a few deep gulps, wiping the glistening remains of the liquid away from the corners of her mouth. She arched her eyebrows and coughed. "Wow, that's strong."

"Yeah, I got it as a gift after I made my debut for the college. We won, I scored a hat trick, and the dean took me aside and told me how proud he was, and that he was sure he had made the right decision in convincing me to come here. I told him that I was going to save it for when I won a championship with a pro team or some other special occasion but, well, screw that. Might as well just have it now," I said, and gestured for her to give it back. We continued in this rhythm, passing the whiskey back and forth as we talked, letting the haze rise within our minds. I was glad that I was sitting down as I had a feeling that my head was going to spin if I stood up.

"You haven't been beaten up again, have you?"

I chuckled dryly. "No, not since the last time. I think that was just a warning."

"A warning for what."

I shot a look at her and shook my head. "I'm not that drunk, Angel. That secret is going with me to the grave."

"But why, I just don't get why you're being so secretive about this. Why won't you tell anyone what happened? Is it really that bad?"

"It's not that it's bad, it's just that it's not my secret to tell, that's all," I said, and hoped that would be the end of it. To make sure I decided to change the topic again. "So, what does this Tommy even want?"

A dark look spread across Angel's face. She took another long drink and finally moved to her bed, where she flopped down on her stomach.

"He says he wants to get back together. He said that he made a mistake and when he learned that he was being kicked out of college there was no other choice in his mind than coming here. He wanted to be with me again and wants to make up for lost time. He thinks he can change and be better and he thinks that we're meant to be together, and that when we're old and grey, we'll look back on this time of our lives and it won't matter at all."

I shook my head again in disbelief. "What a jerk. If there's one thing, I've learned it's that people don't change their patterns. He's not going to change now. I bet if you went out with him, you'd still find him cheating again. That is what he did to you, right?"

"Yeah," Angel said.

I couldn't believe that anyone would cheat on her. She could be stubborn and irascible, but there was something about her that made her sparkle.

"Well, good on you for not falling for his lies. I know, a lot of girls in your position would probably be tempted to give him another chance, you know, trying to believe in the best of him, but you're better off moving on."

"Yeah, but that's part of the problem, as Jeri told me before we went out tonight. I have a problem with moving on. I'm stuck in this limbo where I'm trying to tell myself that he's not important to me, but then I can never bring myself to move on with life. I'm so damned scared of moving forward and dating anyone else, because I'm worried that I'm going to make the same mistake again."

"I know how you feel," I said. She looked at me with surprise in her eyes.

"I felt the same way a lot of time on the ice. You know, if I made a bad play or made the wrong decision, I used to get frustrated with myself, and I didn't know if I would be able to get over it. I used to analyze things a lot to the point where it became unhealthy, and I just had to snap out of it, because it wasn't actually helping me make the right decisions."

"So how did you get over it?"

I shrugged. "I just got used to trusting my instinct again. I told myself that there was something inside me that knew what to do better than my mind did. It took a while, but I was able to act without thinking and then, I was able to see that, just because something didn't go right once, it didn't mean it was going to fail every time."

"I guess that makes sense, but it's a lot different on the ice from in real life."

"I don't know... I think there's a lot you can take from the ice. I'm trying to apply the lessons I learned on the ice to my life now."

"Such as?"

"It's never over until the buzzer goes, there's always a way back into the match, you know, college isn't exactly going well for me right now. I don't know what's going to happen once I graduate. If I graduate," I added the last part in a small voice.

"Are things really that bad? Jeri mentioned you were struggling but..."

"I've never had to be in this position before," I said with a half-smile. "I've always been able to coast along on my talents as a hockey player. Even through high school, I was given help with homework as long as I was able to play. Allowances have always been made for me, but without hockey, I'm nothing and nobody is giving me a helping hand. I'm honestly not sure what I'm supposed to do. I've tried to study. I thought that it was just a matter of time and application, but nothing seems to stick. I'm honestly worried that I'm going to flunk out, and this is all going to be a waste of time."

I sank back and lay flat on my back, staring at the ceiling.

"I'm sorry to hear that, Harry. I didn't know," she said. I heard the pity in her voice. I wasn't sure I liked it.

"Yeah, well, it's just the way it goes. I should have prepared more, I guess. I should have tried harder, shouldn't have made hockey such a big part of my life. I never thought it would go away, you know? Like, it's been a part of me for as long as I can remember and now it's just...

it's just gone. You might think I'm stupid for saying this, but it almost feels as though I've lost a limb or something."

"I felt the same way when things with Tommy ended," she said after she took another sip from the bottle. She cradled it close to her, as though it offered her comfort and stability. I tilted my head up to look at her properly. She gazed into space, as though she was looking into another time. "I used to dream about being with him, you know? I was a stupid little schoolgirl with a stupid schoolgirl crush," she laughed in a self-deprecating tone. "But even though I knew it at the time, I didn't want it to stop. I used to think about him every night and what our lives would be like if we were together. I built it all up in my head, and then, when it turned out he liked me too, I was happier than I'd ever been. It was as though my life finally made sense, you know? Like I had done all I needed to do. I'd found my soul mate, and the only thing left for me to do was to be happy. But then, he went and broke my heart, and I realized that what he offered wasn't paradise at all, it was only an illusion. Now I have nothing too," she said.

Our eyes locked and, in that moment, we realized that we had something in common, something deep and profound. Angel and I had never spent much time together, certainly not by ourselves, but that was the moment when something changed.

"Here's to nothing," I said, taking the bottle from her and drinking a toast to our mutual despair. Was there anything that could unite people more than shared despair?

"So, what are you going to do? I know that Jeri is pretty worried about you, and I can't imagine what your parents think," she asked.

"Oh, they're going crazy. They're scrambling, telling me that I should transfer to another college or that I should just drop out now and start getting in touch with some amateur teams just to boost my reputation. They're acting like it's the end of the world. It's the only thing that's making me glad I'm here. I know that if I was at home, they'd be driving me up the wall."

"They can be pretty intense," Angel said, and we both laughed. It turned out that, when she had whiskey in her, she was quite pleasant company. There had always been an edge between us, but in our solace, we were able to ignore that.

"That's putting it mildly. I still remember when I was a kid, they used to keep me on the ice for hours and hours. It's a wonder I still love the sport as much as I do, considering how much they forced me to play."

"That sounds awful. I had no idea they were like that."

"Oh yeah, it was never ending with them. I guess I can't blame them, considering how far I came, but there are times when I wish I had been a normal child. I know Jeri doesn't feel this way, but she was pretty lucky to be able to hang out with you and do all the things kids do."

"No wonder you were in a bad mood all the time," she said.

"Yeah…" I laughed sheepishly. "I know I was a bit of a jerk. I'm sorry. I guess I just felt jealous of you and Jeri."

"You were more than jealous. You used to call me a nerd. You used to tell me that what I wore was stupid. You were actually pretty nasty to me," she said this in a light tone, with even a hint of a laugh, but I could sense the sadness and pain behind it all. I reflected on my behavior and knew that I had never been that kind to her, but I didn't realize it had affected her so badly. I guess that was the problem with having all my focus on hockey; I lost sight of how other people felt.

"I'm sorry," I said, this time with more sincerity. She took the bottle back from me and took a sip. I had no idea whether that meant she accepted my apology or not.

"I never thought I'd hear you apologize for that. I guess it might just be the whiskey talking," she said, and sighed before I could say anything else. "What is it with men and apologies? Sometimes they can come out so easily, too easily. Tommy apologized a lot, and I don't think he ever meant them."

"Yeah, well, Tommy isn't exactly the measure by which I'd judge other guys."

"What do you mean?"

"I told you before, he's a jerk."

"Yeah, and I told you thanks for letting me know at the time."

"Would you have believed me? Besides, it wasn't my place to interfere. You should just try and ignore him."

"Do you have any idea how difficult it is to ignore an ex after what he did? People act as though cheating isn't a big deal, like it happens so much that you should just be able to get on with things, but I can't. It's horrible, Harry. It makes me feel sick inside. I don't feel like myself. I know he's a jerk, but I loved him. He took that love, and he just threw it away. How am I supposed to cope with that?"

"I don't know," I said sadly. "Relationships aren't exactly my specialty." They were things that had always been easier for other people, but for me they were exotic and unusual. The flings I'd had were never more than that, always fleeting things that evaporated as quickly as dew on a scorching summer's day. A cheer erupted from the met. I scrambled up to the window; Jeri's bed was propped against the window. From this vantage point, I could see the faint glow of the big screen, although I couldn't make out the picture clearly because it was obscured by trees. Angel threw herself on the bed beside me, sitting so close that her shoulders pressed against me. I breathed in the scent of her light perfume. It was flowery and sweet, and contrasted with the hot smell of the whiskey. I glanced towards her, noticing the way her lips were soft as rose petals, and how small dimples formed on her cheeks when her lips twitched into a smile. There were all these small details that I hadn't noticed before and yet now seemed to define her in my mind, like a cluster of three freckles on her collar bone that looked like a constellation, or the hollow of her throat. It was all so intoxicating and new. I was seeing her in a way that I had never seen her before, that I had seen few girls because I had never allowed myself to.

But it was also Angel, my sister's best friend, a girl who had hated me for most of her life.

I tore my gaze away and focused on the outside.

"It must be killing you, knowing they're playing and winning by the sounds of it." Her words were slightly slurred by the drink, but not as slurred as mine were.

"It is. I know I should be out there, that I would be out there if it wasn't for…" I trailed away, knowing that I had almost said too much.

"If it wasn't for what?" she asked, in a voice so quiet it was even less than a whisper. I turned towards her and gazed in her eyes. It might have been the whiskey talking, but there was a part of me that wanted to tell her the truth more than anything in the world. I was so tired of everyone treating me as the enemy. I just wanted one person to know the truth, but I couldn't.

"I'm sorry Angel, I can't," I said.

Angel closed her eyes and sighed. "I really thought you were going to tell me then."

"I thought I might too. Can I tell you a secret? I'm tired of everyone whispering about me and spreading rumors. It's not fun being the bad guy on campus."

"Then tell the truth. Surely you could talk to whoever you're protecting to ask if you can tell some of the truth? It doesn't make sense to me to keep this lie going," she said.

"Maybe… but I'm starting to think I should just leave and go back home. Maybe Mom and Dad are right. Maybe I should try my luck in the amateur league. I'm pretty sure that I'm just failing at college anyway, so what's the use in trying?"

"Don't say that." I was surprised by the urgency in her voice. "Jeri wouldn't be able to handle that. She's always been so proud of you. All she wants is for you to succeed," Angel said.

"But I can't do anything here. I'm no good to anyone. I'm just taking up space and failing slowly."

"Well, if you wanted something to do, you could help me out. It might even make up for the way you bullied me when I was younger." I arched an eyebrow and listened to what she had in mind. "I've had this plan. When Tommy came back, I told him that I had a boyfriend. I thought it would stop him from thinking that we were going to get back together, but he sees it as a challenge and if he finds out I'm lying, then it's just going to make me look immature. I wanted someone to pose as my boyfriend for a while, just to show him that I've moved on and that I don't need him, but so far, nobody has been willing to give it a try. If you wanted something to do then maybe you could be the man I'm looking for?"

I was surprised that nobody had agreed to be her fake boyfriend before, but I guess maybe the guys she asked weren't willing to settle for anything less than the real thing. It wasn't a normal thing to ask, and if it was anyone but Angel, I might have just shaken my head and declined straight away. I couldn't deny it held a certain level of appeal for me though. Besides, Angel did have a reputation as one of the most desirable women on campus. She was intelligent and well liked by the professors, and if people thought we were going out, it might do wonders for my reputation around the college as well.

There was another cheer in the distance, muted by our vantage point, and all I could think about was how I was missing out on so many things I was used to. If being with Angel made people think about me the way they used to think about me, then it might be worth it.

"I'll do it," I said. We smiled at each other, and relief crossed her face. Our eyes locked again and for a moment it felt like we were the only two people in the world. I could feel something stirring inside me, but I wasn't entirely sure what it was. There was a slight tingling feeling in the back of my mind and my gaze fell to her lips, which were alluring. But there was so much history between us I dared not do anything reckless, especially when my head was spinning and when all I really wanted to do was sleep.

Chapter Twelve

Angel

I had been infuriated when Harry of all people turned up on my doorstep and threw himself down on Jeri's bed as though he belonged there. I was surprised at how quickly I had dried my tears, and how long we had spoken. I guess the whiskey helped, but it also helped that we were at the lowest ebbs of our lives. I had been mistreated by the man I loved, and he had been mistreated by the sport he loved. We had given our hearts and souls to these things and had both ended up alone, and it must have been this that bonded us. I never expected to actually enjoy spending time with him, but it was clear this was not the Harry I was used to. He was a man of depth, of pain, and I was really surprised to hear that he didn't have much experience in romance. I never realized how focused he had been.

As we knelt by the window, and I asked him whether he would be my fake boyfriend, our eyes met and I thought something might happen. I almost thought he was going to kiss me, and I tried to ignore the flash of dismay that entered my heart when he didn't. Logically, Harry might well have been the perfect guy to be my fake boyfriend as there was no chance of us developing feelings for each other. I dismissed whatever edge there was in that moment, ascribing it to the effects of the whiskey. My mind was hazy, and I was getting sleepy. We sank to the bed and finished off the bottle, talking about everything and nothing. My limbs grew heavy as did my eyelids, and soon enough there was nothing but darkness.

*

"What the hell is this?" Jeri shrieked.

I was awoken by the shrill sound of her voice. Thunder crashed in my mind as I opened my eyes. The bright light of the morning shone through and blinded me as I opened them. I looked down and saw Harry's body beside mine. A sheet was draped over us, but we were still fully clothed, and thank God for that. I moaned incoherently as I tried to regain my senses. Harry seemed to be in the same state, while Jeri towered above us.

"Is this really what I think it is, and in my own bed too? You can't just leave things alone, can you? You're both as bad as each other," she continued to yell. "I can't believe that you left me last night to come here and sleep with my brother. I thought that you were my friend."

"I am, Jeri. It's not what you think," I managed to force out, although it was hard because the hangover was making it difficult to think straight, and Jeri's war path didn't make it any easier.

"And you," she turned her ire towards Harry, glaring at him with a look that would have killed him a thousand times over if it could. "How dare you do this to me. I try and help you. I do everything I can to make things better for you, and then you make me look like a fool. You come to her?" she pointed to me as though I was a common whore.

"Jeri, this isn't what you think. I can explain," I said, but Jeri wasn't having any of it. She threw up her hands and stormed out of the room, her heavy footsteps receding in the distance. I threw off the cover and went to run after her, but Harry pulled me back.

"She's upset. You should give her some time alone," he said. I wrested myself from his grasp because I knew my friend, but as soon as I got up my head spun, and I felt nauseous. I lost all my equilibrium and fell to the ground. Harry was there to catch me, preventing me from hitting my head. I gasped in pain and clutched my stomach, hating that my body had betrayed me.

"Maybe we should get something to eat as well, to help settle our stomachs. I don't think either of us are in a fit state to move," he said. "Jeri is going to be fine. She's not the type of person to do anything reckless. She probably just needs some time to calm down. This is all just a misunderstanding. It's going to be fine."

I groaned and another wave of nausea hit when I tried to move. There was no hope of me going after Jeri right now even if I wanted to, although I hated the fact that I was stuck like this. I didn't want her to think less of me and I didn't want her to be angry with me. I had never seen a look like that in her eyes before, but something else struck me as well; she was wearing the same clothes as the night before. She had stayed out all night. Was it possible she had met someone?

*

In time, Harry and I got up and walked outside groggily. Every step I took still felt as though it was a risk, as though I was going to empty the contents of my stomach, but I had to try and find Jeri eventually. We went to a café on campus and got a sandwich, as well as a couple of bottles of water to help hydrate our dry mouths. I felt better afterwards, although Harry still seemed the worse for wear.

"If you feel like this every time, I don't understand why getting drunk is so popular," he groaned.

"It's a trade off for the buzz you get at the time," I explained. I looked around to see whether Jeri was anywhere to be seen, but it looked as though I was going to have to hunt for her. Everyone seemed to be in a good mood though, so I assumed that the team won the game. Harry didn't mention anything along those lines.

"So, what we spoke about last night, do you still want me to help you out?"

I paused for a moment, considering the matter, but then I nodded. It wasn't going to be easy, but I didn't want Tommy to think that he had gotten one over on me. "I think we should give it a go at least," I said.

"So how is this supposed to work?" he asked. "Like, what kind of things do you want us to do together?"

"I don't know, I guess just go on dates and act like a couple on campus. I just want word to get around to Tommy that I'm seeing someone, that's all."

"It's not going to do me any harm for people to know that I have a girlfriend either. This could work out well for both of us."

I hadn't considered that fact before. Harry had a reputation to rebuild. He was the one guy on campus who almost needed this as much as I needed it.

"What are the ground rules?" he asked.

"Well, I think the main one is no funny stuff, I mean, at the end of the day this is a fake relationship," I said in a low voice, trying to be as secretive as I could.

"But it needs to be believable, right?" he asked.

"Well, yeah, so I guess we can hold hands and you can put your arm around me and stuff, but I don't want anything to get too affectionate."

I'd known him all my life, so I suppose it was easier to think about being close with him than a stranger, but then again, we had a lot of baggage as well and I wasn't sure how easy it was going to be to get over that. He had been my enemy for so long, was it even possible for him to be my love, even a fake one?

"That's fair enough. You might have to give me some reminders on types of dates and things. Like I said, it's been a long time since I've done anything like this."

"How long?" I asked.

Harry squirmed in his seat, and I have to admit there was a part of me that enjoyed watching him squirm. Even though he had apologized for the way he had treated me when we were younger, the pain stung, and I wasn't ready to let go of it all yet.

"The beginning of last year. I met a girl and we hit it off, thought it was going to be something pretty special, but then hockey got in the way of everything again, like it always did. I guess, at least, that's not going to be a problem here," he said, half-laughing, but I could tell there was a lot of pain in his eyes.

"I guess not," I said. I wondered whether spending more time with him would bring him closer to revealing the secret that he held close to his chest. He had been so close to telling me the truth last night, and I so badly wanted him to tell me what was going on. We smiled shyly at each other after making this pact, unsure of what to say next, unsure of what to do. My gaze drifted away from him towards the entrance of the café as I saw a familiar face. Two familiar faces in fact. My heart sank and this strange eerie feeling came over me, something was terribly wrong. I felt as though the world had spun away from its axis and was hurtling towards the sun.

"Oh my God," I gasped, mouth agape, eyes wide with horror as I saw Jeri enter the café. She wasn't alone. She had been gone all night. It was so unlike her... I almost couldn't believe what I was seeing.

"Wow, Jeri actually broke out of her comfort zone. Good for her," Harry said.

"No, it's not good at all," I said, my heart trembling as I spoke. "The guy she's with... he's my ex."

Chapter Thirteen

Angel

I stared at them, and I didn't know what to think. How could Jeri do this to me? How could she do it to herself? Tommy had his arm around her waist, displaying to the world that he had laid a claim to her. She stayed close to him, pressing her body as close to his as possible and the look in her eyes... I knew that look well. It was the same look that had lingered in my eyes for a long time. The doting, devoted look that made fools of us all. There was a glow around Jeri, the aura of lust shared, and it made me sick to my stomach to think that my best friend had slept with my ex. Questions railed through my mind. I didn't understand any of this. My face paled and I suddenly felt hungover again.

"What do you mean he's your ex?" Harry asked in a hushed whisper.

"What do you think I mean? That's him. That's the guy who hurt me so much. Jeri knows it all. Why would she... how could she...?" It didn't make any sense to me. I continued to stare at them. Jeri threw her head back and laughed at something Tommy said. Her eyes sparkled with excitement the same way mine used to. Tommy had cast his spell on her just as he had enchanted me all those years ago. I thought Jeri would have been more sensible. I thought she would have understood that she shouldn't let herself be his victim. How could she do this to herself? Within moments she had taken her gaze from Tommy and turned it back towards me, and I don't think I'll ever forget that baleful gaze. I saw something in her eyes that I had never seen before. It was malevolent and cruel, and these weren't things I would have ever associated with Jeri. She curled her mouth into a smirk as though she was goading me and narrowed her eyes. She had the triumphant look of a champion, and she slunk away on Tommy's arm.

"Should we go and talk to her?" Harry asked.

It took me a long time to answer the question, so long in fact that he had to nudge me to make sure that I was still listening. I shook my head and turned my face away, finding it unbearable to look at them.

"I can't," I said, almost choking on my emotions. "Not when he's here."

We rose from the table and left. I staggered out of the café in a daze. The world was spinning out of my control, and I had no idea how to handle it. Harry asked me whether I wanted him to stick around and hang out some more, but I needed to be alone. I needed to try and figure this out. I walked back to my dorm, and I waited for Jeri to return, for my best friend to come back to me. She was the last person I thought would ever betray me, and it made me feel sick.

*

It was a couple of hours later when she came back. She walked with a confidence that she had never possessed before. Her face had a hard edge to it that seemed unnatural because I was used to her being so kind and generous with her emotions. She closed the door behind her and stood with one hand on her hip. She arched an eyebrow towards me.

"Well?" she said, expecting me to say something. She radiated hostility. I was on my bed, feeling small and bereft. I gnawed on my lower lip and tried to find the right words. So many things had whirled through my mind that I wasn't sure where to begin, so I started with the simplest question.

"Why?" I asked.

Jeri furrowed her brow. "What do you mean 'why?' I could ask you the same thing. What the hell were you doing with my brother?"

"Nothing."

"Oh really, so the fact that I come back and find you in bed together means nothing, does it? Come on, Angel, I thought you hated him? Have you really sunk so low?"

"It's not like that, Jeri. If you just let me explain-"

"Go on then. I'm listening. Explain to me why you left me alone out there to come back and hang out with Harry. Am I so low on your list of priorities that you'd prefer to hang out with a guy you hate rather than me?"

"What? That's got nothing to do with it. I came back here because I couldn't handle being around Tommy. I wanted to be alone and that's what I intended, but then Harry showed up looking for you and we got to talking. We had a little something to drink and we just decided that we'd rather have some company than be alone. But trust me, nothing happened, nothing like what you're implying anyway. Come on Jeri, it's Harry, why would I do something like that?"

"I don't know, because you're sad?"

"I wouldn't sleep with someone just because I'm sad," I bit back, anger flaring inside me as I wondered how she dared suggest something like this. "It's not like that at all. We just got to talking and he's going to be my fake boyfriend. I know it might not make sense given our history, but he's the only person who could possibly be my fake boyfriend and make it work."

Jeri rolled her eyes and folded her arms across her chest. "Oh great, so now you're roping my brother into this weird plan. Don't you ever just stop and think that what you're doing is crazy? I mean, why are you spending so much time when you could just get on with your life? I've been thinking a lot about this, and it just doesn't make sense. If you were really over Tommy, then I don't think you'd be acting like this. I think you're still in love with him."

I felt as though I had been sucker punched. I visibly recoiled and stared at her, stunned. "How can you say that?"

"Because it's obvious, even if you don't know it yet. You wouldn't have this much of a visceral reaction if he meant nothing to you. Maybe he's right. Maybe there's a part of you that wants to be with him again and you're just trying to do anything you can to convince yourself otherwise. If he didn't matter to you then why would you care about making him jealous?"

"I care because he thinks that he can win me back and I want to prove to him that it's impossible. You should know that better than anyone. And, while we're on the subject, what the hell are you doing acting like that with him? Did you spend the night with him? Did you sleep with him?" My voice rose higher and higher in pitch as I continued to speak, and my heart beat more rapidly.

That same smirk that had appeared in the café was on her face again. "Yes, I did," she said.

I almost threw up there and then.

"How could you?" I asked, the question coming out of my mouth in a wheezing gasp, as though I had been punched in the gut. I stared at her, utterly helpless. She might as well have plunged a knife in my back for the way I felt.

"I can't actually believe you're so surprised. This is what I've been trying to tell you, Angel; you've been so wrapped up in your own problems that you haven't cared about anyone else. Sometimes I think you're incapable of it. What you did last night was unforgiveable."

"What I did? I didn't even screw Harry!" I said, incensed.

Jeri rolled her eyes. "Not Harry. Earlier. When you left me."

I thought back to that moment on the Met when I had turned away and fled from the game. But I didn't understand why that had made her so upset. "What do you mean?"

Jeri let out a dry laugh and shook her head. A few strands of hair fell across her face. "This is exactly what I'm talking about. I was really looking forward to last night. I thought it was going to be a good way for us to have some fun and relax and just be friends again without having to worry about anything, but you had to go and ruin it."

"I didn't ruin anything! Tommy did."

"No, Tommy just happened to be there. You were the one who decided to leave me there all alone. We could have gone and sat somewhere else. You could have put your own feelings aside for a few hours, and put up with Tommy being there, rather than being overwhelmed like every other time. You could have actually thought, 'oh I find this hard, but I know how important it is for Jeri, and how much stress she's been under recently, so I'm going to try and endure it for one night for her sake', but you couldn't do that, could you? Once again it was all about you. You were sad so you walked away. That's all there is to it. You had to put your feelings first again."

"What? No that's not... that's not what happened. I wasn't being selfish. You know what being around Tommy does to me. You know how much I'm affected by what he did. When I see him, I just go into panic mode."

"Yeah, and that's not a healthy reaction, Angel. This is what makes me think that there are still some lingering feelings there. But the fact is that we went out last night together. I put a lot of effort into looking nice, and I wanted to enjoy the game and perhaps meet some new people, and maybe start to enjoy life for once. Recently, you know things haven't been great. I've been helping you cope with this Tommy thing, and then I've been helping Harry cope with his drama. Do you really think this is what I want to be doing with my time? Do you think this is what I came to college for? I don't want to look back on my time with regret either. I've tried to be a good friend and a good sister, but when it came time for you to come through for me you couldn't. You ran away like a scared child, and left me standing there alone, looking like a fool. Do you know how humiliating it was to be left standing there in the middle of the field, with everyone looking at me? It was already hard enough because people know that I'm Harry's sister, so I had to deal with people whispering around me, but again you didn't think of that, did you? You felt bad so you left, and you didn't care one bit what was going to happen to me."

"I... I just needed to leave. I needed to get out of there. I couldn't be around him. It wasn't anything to do with you. I'm sorry, Jeri. You know that I'd never want you to feel that way."

"You say that, but then again you keep acting this way, Angel. Maybe it's my fault because we've been in this relationship for so long. I've always been the one to support you. I've always been the sidekick. Life happens to you and I'm the one who's there to pick up the pieces, but I never get to feel like I'm living life to the fullest. I never feel like I'm the star of my own show, or the main character of my own story, and do you know how depressing that is? When I came to college, I wanted to discover new aspects of myself. I wanted to break free of the person I've grown up as and become something more, and you know what? I hate saying this but, honestly, there are times when I wished that we had gone to different colleges, because I don't feel like I can ever be more than myself when you're around. I'm always going to be that same sad girl who holds you while you cry over a boy, wondering when it's going to be my turn. It's the same with Harry. All my life, I've been second best. I've been the one who just gets on with things, while other people get the excitement and the drama, and I'm tired of it. I don't want to leave college never having experienced something, Angel. I don't want to keep getting told that it's all going to work out for me eventually, because that's not how life works. So, when you left me last night, I finally realized that I don't matter to you as much as your feelings matter. You just left me and what was I supposed to do, come back running so that I could comfort you again? Is that what you expected of me?"

I turned my face away in shame as the words thundered out of her mouth. There was more truth to what she said than I cared to admit. It certainly wasn't a conscious decision on my part, but we had fallen into certain roles, and perhaps I had taken her for granted over the years. I felt horrible, because part of me had expected her to come back with me.

"You're right Jeri. I'm sorry," I said, meeting her gaze so that she could see the earnestness in my eyes. She was a little taken aback by the readiness with which I apologized. "I haven't always been a good friend to you and it's not fair. You have always been there for me, and I'm sorry that I've let myself fall into this role. You're right; you do deserve to have a better friend and you do deserve to be the star of the show. You're a great person. I've always said that. I was looking forward to last night as well, but when I see Tommy, this switch goes off inside me and something happens that I can't control. I just feel like the world is spinning and I can't get my balance again. I get scared, terrified, and all I want to do is run away. You're probably right that it's not healthy, and I don't want it to continue. I want to be better, Jeri, and I want to be a better friend as well, but I still don't understand how you could be with him, after everything he's done," I gazed at her with disbelief, and there was a hint of an accusing tone. "Did you do it just to get back at me? Was this some weird way for you to prove to yourself that you can get the same guys as I can?"

Jeri barked a laugh again. "Angel, not everything is about you. What happened is that Tommy came up to me and spoke to me like a human being. He invited me to come and sit with his friends, and he spoke to me about college and the game and pretty much everything else. We sat there for hours and hours just talking, and not once did you come up. Do you know how refreshing it is? It's funny because it never seemed like Tommy is far from your mind, but he didn't mention you at all. He asked about me because he's interested in me. We had a few drinks, and all of his friends were nice. It was a good time, the kind of time that I missed out on when I was comforting your tears. And after the game was over, he invited me back to his room. I thought about it for a long time. My first instinct was to say no because I knew how you were going to feel about it. I was worried about you, and I wanted to check on you, but then I realized that's the exact thing I've been doing all my life. So, I thought this time I'd try something different.

We went back to his dorm, and he put on some music. We had a little bit to drink, and I started to wonder whether he was really as bad as you said. He told me how difficult it had been to be in a long-distance relationship and how hard it was when he was such a tactile person. Then, he started kissing me and I let him. It felt nice, and even though he's your ex, I thought maybe just this once she won't mind because I'm not her and it might not end the same way with Tommy, and maybe I might even be a better girlfriend because I know how to make people feel better."

"I can't believe you're saying this," I replied, wincing as she mentioned a few details about the previous night. When I learned that Tommy had cheated on me, I hated thinking about him with the other girls, knowing they had been lurking in the background while we had been speaking on the phone, knowing that he was drowning in a sea of lust with them moments after he told me that he loved me and missed me. But now I hated thinking about Jeri being with him, knowing that she had been charmed by the devil and she was too blind to see it. "This isn't you, Jeri."

"No, it's not, and I don't think that's a bad thing. In fact, I'm quite liking this new me."

I shook my head in disbelief. "You know that it's all lies, don't you? Whatever he's been telling you, he doesn't mean any of it. It's all going to end the same way."

"No, it's not," she said, and the conviction in her voice worried me. "It's not because I'm not you. I'm going to prove to you that I'm better at holding on a man than you are. I can give Tommy something you didn't. I can make him love me. The thing is, Angel, that you spent so long building him up inside your head, that you couldn't appreciate the real thing. People aren't perfect. Your standards were too high and how was he supposed to live up to that?"

I was shocked again at how she was parroting his words. "You sound just like him," I said, forlorn because it felt as though I was literally losing my friend.

"You just don't like it because it's not something you want to hear. You don't like being told you're wrong, Angel, but I should have given you some home truths a long time ago. You need to move on from Tommy and you need to understand that I'm going to live my life the way I want to live it, and it doesn't matter if I do anything you disapprove of because you don't have that kind of power over me."

"I don't want that kind of power, Jeri. I just don't want you to make the same mistakes I did. I don't want you to fall for his lies because that's exactly what you're doing."

"You're wrong," she said with another dry laugh. "I mean a lot to Tommy. We have something special and, just because things ended badly with you, doesn't mean the same is going to happen with me. You're just going to have to live with it because I'm not going to live my life to make you feel better or anything like that."

"I don't want you to, Jeri. I'm worried about you. Why couldn't it be anyone but Tommy? There are so many other guys on campus. Why him?"

"I could say the same thing to you about Harry. But while you're going to be off having this fake relationship, I'm going to be having a real one, so think about that when you wonder why you're unhappy. I'm actually willing to take a risk in life. I'm not going to be frozen in fear like you. And don't worry, I'm not going to let your secret slip to Tommy. The truth is that you don't really matter as much to him as you think you do. I'm the one he cares about now, and I tell you what, it feels pretty good," she said. There was nothing more I could say. She gathered some clothes and then stormed out, saying that she was going to hang out at Tommy's for a little while so I could be alone in my misery, because apparently, that's clearly what I wanted. I watched her leave in silence, barely able to believe that this was really happening.

Chapter Fourteen

Angel

"I feel like I should have said something else or done something to make her stay and see that what she's doing is crazy," I groaned as I sat on Harry's bed, holding my head in my hands. I had just described to him what happened between Jeri and me, and he had a pensive look on his face.

"I can't believe things were that bad. I knew she was struggling with what happened, but I didn't realize she was this upset. I wish I had done more as well. I think maybe she has a point. Maybe we've both been a little too involved with our own problems," he said.

"She did say that we had more in common than we might think," I replied. It was supposed to lighten the mood, but somehow it didn't succeed. "I just don't know what to do now. I feel like I can't let her be with Tommy, not when I know what he's capable of. Jeri should know better. It's all going to end in tears, and I don't know whether I'm going to be there when it all happens."

"Is it going to end in tears though? I know that what Tommy did to you was terrible and I never had a good feeling about him myself, but is there definitely no possibility that he might genuinely like Jeri?"

I considered the matter for a moment, but then dismissed it almost immediately. "No way. If Jeri thinks I'm self-involved then she has no idea what she's getting herself into with Tommy. He's the most self-involved person I've ever known. He only ever uses people for his own ends. I wouldn't be surprised if he's just using Jeri to get back at me. Once he's done with her, he'll toss her aside like everyone else, and she's going to be so hurt. I need to do something to save her. I need to talk to her again or speak to Tommy. I hate the idea, but maybe it's just something I need to do for Jeri's sake. Maybe I can convince him to break up with her before he hurts her too much."

"I don't think that's a good idea," Harry said in a low, slow voice. I stared at him as though he was crazy.

"What do you mean it's not a good idea? We have to do something. I'm not going to stand by and let her make the biggest mistake of her life."

Harry sighed and shrugged. "Maybe that's exactly what we should do. Jeri has earned our trust. She's always been there for us and maybe, what she really needs now is our support. If we try and interfere, it's only going to get her more annoyed with us, and if you try and break her and Tommy up, she's going to be more determined to stay with him."

"Don't you want to stop her from getting hurt?"

"I do, but I'm also thinking about how she's going to feel in the long run. We've both taken her for granted, Angel, and I think she's earned the right to make her own mistakes. This is her choice, and we have to respect that if we really care about her, even though it might all end in tears. But at least, she'll have learnt for herself. And then, we'll be there to pick up the pieces. But if you go charging in, she's only going to get angrier and she's going to think that you don't trust her. I think this is one of those situations where we just have to stand back and see how things unfold. It's like in hockey when-"

I glared at him and held up a palm to silence him. "Please don't use another hockey analogy. I don't think I can take that right now." I felt warm all over. All I wanted was to save my friend from the inevitable heartbreak that Tommy would cause, but what Harry said made sense. Anything I did to interfere would only drive her away and probably make her more convinced that I was still in love with Tommy. Nothing was further from the truth of course. It was clear that he was already twisting her mind and fashioning truths from lies. Just the thought of him whispering in her ear made me so angry, I was about ready to burst. I rose abruptly from the bed and kicked out at the chair by his desk.

"I need to get out of here," I declared.

"Well how about we go on our first fake date?" he suggested. I wasn't even sure now that this whole fake boyfriend thing was a good idea, but since we had already agreed to it, I figured we might as well.

"Sure," I said, and we left his dorm.

*

Despite the fact that this fake boyfriend thing was supposed to show Tommy that I had moved on from him, Harry and I decided that we wanted to get away from the campus for a while. He drove us out to a strip where there was a cinema, a mini golf course, and a range of cool and chic stores that had unusual things inside. There were plenty of other people about and it felt good to escape from the campus bubble for a little while. Sometimes it was easy to forget that a world existed outside college.

"I'm going to get one of those," Harry said, his eyes widening when he saw a burger truck. He sped over there at such speed it was difficult for me to catch up. He was wearing a pale blue top that was stretched over his athletic physique. I noticed a few girls staring at his biceps. They shot me envious glances as I walked closer to Harry, and I have to admit it felt good. When I joined him at the counter, I found him ordering a burger with pretty much everyone on it. He asked me whether I wanted anything, so I got a plain cheeseburger.

"I don't feel like stuffing my arteries with cholesterol today," I said.

Harry just grinned. "I've never had something like this before, so I think I might as well try one now," he licked his lips as he was handed a greasy burger that was swollen with ingredients to the point where it was fit to burst. I don't think I'd ever seen a man as happy as Harry when he took his first bite. "Oh my God that's good," he said. "I can't believe I haven't had one of these before."

"Neither can I. Has your diet always been this strict?"

Harry nodded, murmuring through mouthfuls. "Pretty much. Mom and Dad always told me that if I wanted to be a pro then I had to act like one from the very beginning. They said that it was good to form positive habits from a young age, and that I would appreciate the sacrifice in the long run. Sometimes it was a drag, but I guess I've been doing it for so long that I didn't think it was anything other than normal. But now that I've tasted this… oh wow," he attacked the burger with real intent, savagely biting so that ketchup and mustard coated his lips and burst out all over the napkin and his hands. I couldn't help but laugh.

"I think you should be glad that this is a fake first date. If this is what you've done on other dates then I'm not surprised that none of your relationships have lasted."

He took a moment to look down at himself and the mess he had created, and then he laughed too. "Yeah, well I guess it helps that you know me already. To be honest I think I might do this on a normal first date as well. It's better that someone knows what they're getting themselves into," he smirked, and we both laughed. He finished the burger and we continued walking around the stores, peering into windows and idly looking at everything they had to offer.

"So what else have you been deprived of?" I asked.

"That's kind of a hard question to ask. I don't really know what I've missed out on because I haven't done it. But it's little things, like hanging out after dark, going for long drives, indulging in a takeaway now and then. I mean, I haven't even had popcorn at the movies all that often. Everything in my life has been geared towards hockey and now it's just all gone. I'm at a bit of a loose end."

I was touched by the way he seemed so forlorn and lost. When he spoke about hockey, it was as though he spoke of a long lost love that could never be regained. I could sense the regret he had and the wistfulness in his heart, which again made me wonder just what had happened for him to give up the thing he loved the most. I didn't ask him again though, knowing that if I pressed him, he would probably just clam up and refuse to tell me. But if I waited, maybe, it would come naturally.

"Well, I think we can change that. Come on, there's probably a show we can catch now."

We rushed to the cinema and managed to catch a show. Action movies weren't usually my thing, but it was the only thing on, and I figured Harry would probably enjoy it. He stuffed pop corn into his mouth like it was going out of fashion. I laughed, watching him almost as much as I watched the movie. He seemed genuinely happy and free, which was a far cry from the way he had been the other night when he staggered half-drunk into my room. I had to check myself a few moments during the night, because I couldn't believe that I was actually sitting with Harry and having a good time. This guy was my tormentor through childhood, but here I was discovering a new side of him, and I wondered what else I would find.

When the movie was over the lights came on and Harry rubbed his stomach.

"I need to walk for a bit," he said. We left the cinema. By this point, the stores were shutting and most of the people had drifted towards bars. I didn't think having drinks together again was a good idea, so I guided us away from these and enjoyed the cooling breeze that wafted through the air.

"So have you given any thought to what you're going to do if you can't play hockey?" I asked.

Harry sighed. "No. I keep wracking my brains, but I've spent so long training for this one thing there's just nothing else for me. Do you ever feel like you've done life wrong? Like, you've messed things up and now it's too late to ever go back and change it?"

I nodded. "Yeah, mainly with Tommy. I spent so much time wanting him and only him that I missed out on dating other guys. Then, we finally got together, and I thought, if I was patient and loyal and faithful, things would work out and we'd be together in the end.

But that was never going to happen. A lot of guys asked me out, you know, in college I mean. I shot all of them down because I had a boyfriend and then, when I found out Tommy had cheated on me, I really wished that I had done the same thing to him."

"Well, at least the fact you didn't shows that you're a good person."

"I know, but it still makes me wonder whether I'd have found someone who really loved me. Tommy just... didn't. As much as he said it, he never meant the words. And I think I always knew it, or at least I sensed it deep down, I just never listened to that part of me because I didn't want to believe it. But yeah, there are times when I just want to go back in the past and shake myself awake, and yell at myself to not waste so much time with him."

"Can I ask you a question, Angel?"

"Sure."

"This thing with Tommy happened a while back, right? I know you, and I know guys, and I know there have definitely been other guys interested in you since then. Why haven't you gone out with any of them? I mean, wouldn't a real relationship be better than a fake one?"

It was a legitimate question. A knot tightened in my stomach before I answered. I usually only shared these kinds of thoughts with Jeri, although at this point, I didn't know whether our friendship would last. It was a little sad to think that Harry was the only person left in the world with whom I could talk about these things, but there was something about him that made it all seem natural. It didn't seem strange to talk about my feelings. Maybe it was just because we had known each other all our lives, or maybe it was something more...

"The truth is that it probably would be, but after what happened with Tommy, I just get so scared of trusting someone again. Guys have asked me out, and sometimes I've even been tempted to say yes, but then, I start thinking about getting close to them and all I can think about is how Tommy took my trust and wrecked it. It was so devastating that I can't risk it happening again. I'm not sure I could survive it, so I have to be cautious. And I know it's irrational and I've probably missed out on a lot of wonderful experiences, but I feel this ache inside me whenever I get close, and I just can't let this fear go."

"I'm sorry to hear that," Harry said, and I got the sense that he genuinely was. "Well, hopefully this can help then. You know that you can trust me."

"Can I?"

He stopped for a moment as I asked the question. We turned to face each other. Our eyes locked. I noticed the way his chest rose and fell. There was a time when we were children. He had been taller than me even then, always just a little ahead in this race of life. Back then he used to point and laugh and tease me, sending me away in tears. There was a part of that little girl inside me now, but there was also a woman who had grown over the years, and this part of me appreciated the man he had become. Did I trust him? Yes, perhaps despite my better judgment. He had more depth than I realized, more humanity. He had shown me his emotions, bare and naked, and I had shown him mine as well. But I still couldn't shake the fact that, years ago, he had bullied me. For so long now, I had thought of him as the enemy, and it was a hard habit to shake.

"Angel, I wouldn't be here if you couldn't."

"Harry. There's something I need to talk to you about, that I need to ask you. I know we spoke about it a little bit the other night... but why were you so mean to me when we were younger? Why did you treat me so badly?"

There was a sharp intake of breath from Harry as he looked around before his gaze settled on me again. "I was just a stupid kid. I didn't think about what I was doing, I just did it. Looking back now, I was stressed without realizing it. I was under a lot of pressure from Mom and Dad, so I picked on someone weaker than me. And I guess a part of it was that I was jealous that you got to hang out with my sister more than I did. I used to watch the two of you playing as though you didn't have a care in the world, and I wanted to be a part of that. I couldn't take out my frustration on Mom and Dad, so you were the next best target. I know it's not mature or rational and I'm not proud of it. I look back and wish I was better. You didn't deserve it. Even when I used to tease you as a teenager, I asked myself why I was doing it even as it was happening, and I couldn't come up with an answer. I'm sorry, Angel. At the time, I didn't realize how it was affecting you."

I wasn't really sure how to handle his apology. I hadn't ever really expected him to apologize, and I think that moment was the moment when I realized what Jeri had been trying to tell me. I had made this pain a part of myself, a part of my identity, but it wasn't healthy. I could think about the way he treated me all the time and build my history around that, or I could try and be better and think of myself in better terms. It wasn't healthy to hold a grudge like this and to keep dwelling on the past. Harry had bullied me when I was younger, but he wasn't the same man now, and I wasn't the same girl. I didn't have to be the victim and if there was anyone bullying me now, it was myself.

"What are you smiling about?" Harry asked when he noticed me smirking.

"It's nothing really. I think I just started to understand life a little better, that's all."

We strolled along for a little while longer, laughing at childhood memories and sharing stories that neither of us had ever heard before. It was comfortable, and the rhythm of conversation was such that it didn't seem as though it was ever going to end. I honestly thought I could stay with him all night and we'd never run out of things to talk about. It was something I hadn't felt for a long time, and when he walked me back to my dorm, I was unable to wipe the smile from my face. He stood there, framed by the stars.

"This was fun tonight. I'm glad we did it. I guess it's not bad for a fake first date," he said with a grin.

I smiled back and nodded. "It was fun. I think it's what we both needed," I said.

"Good, and now it's your turn to think of the second date."

"Sounds like a deal," I replied. There was a moment where our eyes met, and the air was laced with tension. I tilted my head back a little to meet his gaze. He was such a tall, impressive guy that he filled my vision. My lips parted as he leaned down. His lips brushed my cheek ever so softly. I tingled as I felt the lingering warmth of his breath and then, I was standing there alone, almost wishing that he had kissed me.

I returned to my room confused about what I had just experienced. This was all supposed to be fake, but I couldn't deny that I'd had a good time with Harry. He made me laugh, he made me comfortable enough to share my feelings, and I didn't feel as though he was going to hurt me. I raised my fingers to my lips when I got to my bed, finding myself wondering what it would have been like to kiss him. It was a thought that had never entered my mind before, but I couldn't say that it was entirely undesirable. But there were other things on my mind too; I glanced across at Jeri's bed and found myself wishing she was there. Usually, I would have spoken to her about a date, but instead her bed was empty and she was with Tommy, probably embracing the lies he was telling her about loving her more than he loved anyone else, the same lies he had told me.

I wrapped my arms around myself and forced myself to go to sleep, trying not to think about the strange circumstances that had led to my enemy becoming my fake boyfriend and my best friend becoming my enemy. It was almost too crazy to be real.

Chapter Fifteen

Angel

A few weeks had gone by since Harry and I had started 'dating'. It was going pretty well actually. We had a similar sense of humor and I never felt as though I was going to run out of things to talk about. He had a real lust for life and wanted to enjoy things that had always been denied him, so we did a lot of fun things on and off campus. I helped him with his studies as well, spending time hunched over a desk as he tried to apply himself. I had always seen him as a skilled and confident guy. On the ice, he was a master of his own destiny and there was no doubting his skill, but when he studied, he seemed to be crippled by a lack of confidence, and I almost couldn't believe it was the same man I was used to. I spent a lot of time with him, and I did manage to help him, but it wasn't easy. I realized that I was seeing Harry as I had never seen him before, and I had to admit that I liked what I was seeing. I looked forward to our little dates, and didn't mind when they drifted away into this endless lazy stream of time where nothing seemed to matter. We walked around campus hand in hand, arm in arm, and it didn't feel strange. I know it should have, but it didn't. Harry didn't seem fazed by this either, and it appeared to be working. We noticed more than a few people glancing our way and whispering. Harry didn't suffer any black eyes, although he still didn't tell me what had happened that resulted him in getting off the team, but in truth I had other things to worry about.

While this was going well, I was concerned about my friendship with Jeri. Since she'd started dating Tommy, we had barely seen each other. There were times when I came back from class, I saw that things had been rearranged or a drawer had been left open, so I knew that she had been back to get a change of clothes, but the fact that she did so while I was out, led me to think that she was purposefully avoiding me. I wasn't sure whether I should be worried about this or not. Clearly, she needed space, but how much space was necessary? I know things had ended on bad terms with this, but I didn't think they had ended completely. She was still my best friend. I didn't want this to be the end of us. My heart sank whenever I thought of the prospect, and on this particular day, it was getting me down. Harry was in the middle of telling a story. I guess he reached a point where I should have been laughing, because he pulled me up when I didn't react the way I should have.

"Have we reached the point of this relationship where I'm boring you already?" he asked with a twinkle in his eye. We always joked about our relationship in this way, pretending it was real.

I offered him a weak smile. "No, it's okay, I'm just worried about Jeri, that's all. I thought we'd at least have spoken about this by now, but she's avoiding me. I know you said that we shouldn't get involved and that it's not our business, but I hate to imagine what he's telling her. Tommy is good at making people believe whatever he says, and I dread to think that he's turning her against me. What if we're never friends again?" I asked. My voice trembled and the fear must have been plain to see on my face because he put an arm around my shoulders and squeezed in an effort to reassure me. Familiar, intimate gestures like these had become natural and regular between us, in an effort to present a false image to the world, so I didn't think there was anything strange about his touch. In fact, I found it quite reassuring.

"It's going to be okay. I don't think anything can get in between you two. You've been friends all your life. You've been through so much together. Who could possibly get in the way of that?"

The question was rhetorical, but there was an answer I could have given him, Tommy. There was nothing that man was incapable of, no lows that he wouldn't stoop to.

"I need to speak with her," I said.

"Okay," he said.

I arched my eyebrows towards him. "Are you sure?" I asked.

"If that's what you need to do, then that's what you need to do. Besides, I haven't spoken to her much myself recently, and when I have, the conversations have been brief. I have to admit that I'm a little worried about her."

We walked across campus to Tommy's dorm. Nerves rose in my stomach as we approached his building, but I felt safer knowing that Harry was with me. I nestled into him a little bit and whispered a thank you to him for coming with me. He didn't say anything in reply, merely accepted that this was his place as my 'boyfriend', and I appreciated his support.

Harry knocked on the door. Tommy opened it and chuckled a little at the sight of us. I peered past him, trying my best to ignore the fact that he was there even though I knew it would be a futile effort, but I saw Jeri behind him.

"How nice of you to drop by, Angel. It's been too long since we've bumped into each other, and you must be Harry. Jeri has told me so much about you. Well, don't you make a lovely couple," he said in his silky-smooth voice.

"I didn't come here to talk to you Tommy. I came here to speak with Jeri," I said in a harsh tone.

"Well how rude, but I suppose it's understandable," he said as he stepped aside, leaving the path free and clear to Jeri. She was sitting on the edge of his bed and glared at me.

"What are you doing here?" Jeri asked.

"I came to see you. I'm worried about you because you've been avoiding me. I want to talk to you. I miss you, Jeri."

"Oh really? Because you seem to have been spending a lot of time with Harry. It seems as though you've been having a lot of fun together," Jeri said in a spiteful tone.

"Jeri, come on, there's no need to be like that," Harry said, coming in to stand beside me.

"Don't you even bother talking to me, Harry. After everything I've done for you, and you go and do this? I don't need you siding with her. Don't you remember everything I've done for you over the years."

"Of course I do, Jeri. That's not what this is about. We're not trying to make you do anything and I'm not siding with Angel. We just miss you, that's all," Harry continued.

"No, you're upset because I'm spending more time with Tommy, and you don't like it because for the first time, I'm not under your control anymore. Well, you're going to have to get used to it because Tommy and I are serious. He's not going anywhere."

Harry and I glanced at each other. "Jeri, if you're happy then I'm happy. I just miss you, that's all. I want to hang out with you again."

When Jeri looked at me, it was as though she was a different person. I found the look in her eyes haunting. There was a darkness inside that I had never seen before, and it chilled me to my very core. "So, you can try and tell me what a bad guy Tommy is and how I shouldn't be with him? Yeah, okay, I don't think that's going to happen. I'm my own person, Angel. Harry, you had better take notice of this as well. I don't want either of you interfering in my life. I'm with Tommy and I'm happy. I'm in love. There's nothing you can do or say to change my mind. You need to leave now. Tommy and I want to be alone."

"Jeri, come on, there's no need to be like that," Harry said, taking a step into the room, but Tommy shifted around to block the way. Harry snarled. "Get out of my way."

"I think it's time that you and Angel leave. Jeri has made it clear that she doesn't want to see you right now," Tommy said.

"You can't stop me from seeing my sister."

"I believe I can. This is my room after all, and from what I understand, you're on rather thin ice when it comes to your place in this college. If there's any other misdemeanor, I'm sure the Dean won't have any hesitation in throwing you out, especially if any of the stories I've heard are true." When he said this, Tommy turned his head to look at me directly. "Frankly, Angel I'm surprised that you would let yourself become besotted with this man. Don't you know what he's capable of? Especially after all the things you accused me of... why, I think I'm a saint in comparison."

He smirked, but the smirk was driven from his face as Harry's anger got the better of him. His face twisted with fury, and he grabbed Tommy by his collar and slammed him against the wall, lifting him an inch off the ground. I had seen Harry be mean like this on the ice, but to see it in real life was something frightening.

"You're no saint. I know what you did to Angel, and if you do anything like that to Jeri, I'm going to find you and they're not going to be able to identify what's left behind," he said.

"Harry, get off him!" Jeri yelled. She rose and pulled her brother off Tommy. I was too shocked to move. Tommy cleared his throat and caught his breath, retreating to the rear of the room as Jeri pushed Harry away. I caught him and we stumbled out. The door slammed shut behind us.

*

"I guess that didn't go as planned," Harry said a little while later. We'd returned to my dorm to calm down. Harry was still pacing around the room. I felt empty inside. "I'm sorry for what happened. When he spoke like that I just... I don't know what happened. I just lost it. After everything you told me about him and he just stands there looking so smug, as though he's already won."

"This is just what he does," I said in a broken and cracked voice. I stared into space, feeling the sorrow rising within me.

"I could have punched him right then and there. I understand now how he could drive you so crazy. I couldn't believe the way he spoke to you after all he's done to you, and to think he's doing the same thing to Jeri," Harry's words were heavy and filled with tension. He kept clenching and unclenching his fists as he spoke. I could feel the anger pouring out of him, and the fact he was so defensive of me was astounding. It was the way a real boyfriend would have acted, and I started to wonder if the lines between reality and illusion were being blurred.

He continued speaking, but then I went off on a tangent. Even though I spoke in a whisper it was enough to make him stop and descend to the bed beside me. "I couldn't believe the way she acted. That wasn't the Jeri I know. I'm worried that I've lost her Harry. What if she's never coming back?"

He put his arm around me again, the comforting blanket of warmth that was so soothing and natural. I rested my head against his shoulder as crystal tears trickled down my cheeks.

"It's going to be okay. She's not lost to us. She's still Jeri, and all we can do is keep trying to tell her that we care about her, and show her that we're not angry at her or trying to break her and Tommy up. There's only so much she can do. She's still probably hurting right now and thinking that she needs to do this to teach us a lesson. I'm sure she misses us as well. We just need to give it time."

"But it's all my fault." The more I spoke, the more the sorrow got the better of me. "If I had just listened to her more or paid more attention or been stronger, she wouldn't have done this. If I had just stayed with her that night instead of running back here, Tommy wouldn't have been able to get to her..." I trailed off in sobs. Harry made soft comforting noises and squeezed me even tighter. Warm tears flowed over my lips. I could taste the saltiness in them.

"It's not your fault," he kept repeating over and over, as though if he said it enough, then it would become true, but I knew it wasn't. It was my fault that Jeri had been driven into Tommy's arms. I had been a bad friend, and Jeri was the one who was going to suffer because of it.

I wasn't sure for how long Harry held me, but it was a long time. My body shuddered and I felt so small in his arms, so frail. I imagined myself as a tiny bird made of the finest crystal and was amazed that

Harry was able to hold me so tightly without breaking me. I was able to relax in his arms, knowing that he was a shield around me, protecting me from all the bad things in the world.

I lifted my gaze and met his eyes. My vision was blurred with tears, but I could see him clearly.

"Don't take this the wrong way," I said in a soft voice, "but you're the last person I thought I would ever be comforted by."

He returned my smile. His penetrating gaze was intense. I could feel his fingers pressing against me, nestling against the natural curves of my body. I was lulled by the steady rhythm of his breathing. The longer I gazed into his eyes, the more I realized that I was falling into them, but I wasn't scared at all. I knew that nothing bad could happen because he wouldn't let anything bad happen to me.

With a tender thumb, he wiped the tears away from my eyes, as well as pushing a few errant strands of hair away from my face.

"You know, this has probably been the closest I've ever felt to someone, even if this is a fake relationship. In fact, even though it's fake, it's starting to feel more real all the time."

My heart skipped a beat as he said this. I felt the same way, even though I had been afraid to admit it to myself. While I was there in his arms, it was difficult to imagine ever wanting to be anywhere else. I could feel myself melting into him, losing myself in him, and suddenly I wanted this to be real more than anything. The way he took care of me, the way he laughed, the way everything seemed more exciting when he was around. It might have started off as fake, but now I wanted more.

"I want this to be real," I whispered. It was a secret my heart had spoken.

"Are you sure?" he asked, his face inching closer to mine. The air was warm. My heartbeat was rapid. I nodded, and before I knew it, our lips had pressed together in an intense and fiery kiss.

Chapter Sixteen

The kiss reached into the depths of me and blazed around my body so that I felt I was on fire. His lips were tender and firm, his kiss insistent, and mine yielded underneath the glorious fury of his passion. A soft moan escaped my lips as we stared at each other in amazement, wondering whether this was really happening. My bully, my enemy, now my lover. I reached up and placed a hand against his cheek, smiling at him. I leaned in and kissed him again, closing my eyes to embrace the heavenly feeling that swept through me. We rolled in the bed, locking lips, wrapping limbs around each other as the tension that had been building between us was suddenly unleashed. His breaths were hot and frantic as his hands roamed over my hips and shoulders and arms. His body pressed into me, and I could feel the swell of arousal. There was a twitch in the deepest part of me and my body started to ache. It had been so long since I felt this heat, so long that I wondered whether this part of me even existed anymore. It had taken Harry to bring it back to life.

I ran a hand to the back of his neck and kissed him deeply, thrusting my tongue forward to dance with his. He was seized with masculine desire and nuzzled into me, kissing me down my neck and across my collarbone, tugging at my troublesome clothes, stretching the fabric so taught I thought he was going to rip them all apart. My hands traveled over his huge biceps and his taut back. Despite his recent indulgences, he still had the toned body of an athlete with all the gorgeous majesty that came with it.

There was a moment of disconnect as I realized that I was kissing Harry, but any doubt or eeriness I felt was burned away by the sheer force of passion that blazed between us. Our lips and bodies were locked in this paroxysm of delight. My breaths were lost in a flurry of moans and pants, while his hands were all over me. It felt as though there were a hundred men groping and fondling me, but there was only one, the only one that mattered. He pulled my top over my head as he kissed me. His hands fell around my back and deftly unclasped my bra, letting my breasts pour out. He groaned with delight as he buried himself in me, kissing my soft supple flesh.

I leaned back, offering him the hollow of my throat and groaned as he sucked and nibbled my nipples. Waves of pleasure shot through me, and my eyelids fluttered shut. If he had ended there and then, I would have been happy, but he was only just getting started. I groaned as he descended down my body. He kissed in the valley between my breasts and then kept his hands on them, pinning me to the bed in a display of strength. Every breath I took was laced with pleasure and I became more and more intoxicated by his musky smell of masculinity and sex. Then he was kissing my stomach, and his hands were around my waist, pulling down my skirt and panties in one lusting motion, using all of his strength to leave me naked and exposed. I wriggled to help him, wanting to be free of everything that constrained me. My body ached and yearned and everything inside me wanted to be touched by him. I writhed under his touch and my mouth formed an oval as I felt his lips linger over my skin. He breathed in and his hands dropped down to my thighs, my slick and burning thighs.

I groaned as he dug his hands in and then started kissing me in my most intimate area. His tongue lapped and licked and danced. My eyes rolled in the back of my head, and I gnawed on my lip as I tried to brace myself against the pleasure. I gasped and groaned and touched myself all over, feeling as though I was alive for the very first time. Everything was more vivid and vibrant than it had ever been before, and it was all thanks to him. It was as though he had stripped away something that had been shielding me from the true glory of the world, and it was only thanks to him that I could truly live.

I felt him pleasure me. Waves rippled out, starting in the molten core of my body and expanding to the tips of my fingers and toes.

It was a warm, glowing feeling that radiated through me. My heart thundered and my mind was awash in a cacophony of pleasure. I had never thought of Harry as a tender or passionate man before, but he was a man who tried his best to excel at everything he attempted, and he excelled at this. Sharp breaths burst out of me one after the other and sweat poured down in a torrential flood, beading on my temples and trickling down my breasts, leaving my skin glistening. My thighs burned and as he looked up at me, I could see that his lips were shining with my wetness.

He buried himself against me and I thought he was going to go all night. Pleasure came crashing through me again and again, rising and falling with the rhythm of his tongue. I arched my legs up and clasped his head, holding him in place, loving the way he was making me feel. It was as though he was burning away every iota of doubt and anguish that had laced my heart. I could feel myself soaring and it was all because of him. A hazy, dreamy feeling seized my mind and then rampaged through the entirety of my body, leaving me gasping and drained. It throbbed and pulsed and left me a shuddering wreck on the bed. I felt as though I was going to melt, and I wanted him to feel as good as I did.

I pulled him away, moaning gently that I couldn't take anymore. I hated to admit defeat, but I could feel myself fainting if he continued, such was the overwhelming force of everything he was doing to me. I managed to pull myself up to my knees, although I ended up having to rest against him anyway. He caught me in his arms and smiled, amused at the state of me, but it was all his fault. I pressed myself against his body, loving the safety and the form of his body. I kissed him and tasted myself on his lips. It was sweet. He held me in his arms. My hair cascaded down his arms and across his chest as I reached down, sliding my hand across his thigh towards the bulging arousal that threatened to break free of his pants. A lump formed in my throat, partly fear, partly anticipation as I felt how huge he was. I licked my lips, and he quickly helped my trembling hands to undress him. I watched as the fabric was pulled away. Dark shadowy hair appeared and then his manhood followed, inch by hard inch revealing itself until the smooth, thick tip was in full view. The shaft was long and thick, the smooth, taut skin wrapped with rippling veins around it. My eyes widened and desire flared within me.

I dropped down and ran my hand around it, feeling the warmth scorch my fingers. He brushed thick handfuls of hair away from my face as I looked up at him, wanting to see the look on his face as I pleasured him. He towered above me. Every muscle was on full display. His face was tense and twisted in a pleasured snarl. His hand was against the back of my head, holding me in place as I descended on his erection, leaving a trail of saliva coating it. I gasped for breath as I stretched my jaws to take every inch. I breathed in all the arousing smell of his manly musk and gorged myself on him. I swirled my tongue around and stroked him as I sucked, unable to help soft and sharp moans from bursting out of my mouth. I had never wanted a guy this much, not even Tommy, not this primally, not this savagely. I wanted him to take every part of me and do anything he wanted with me. I wanted his hands all over me.

I wanted him.

Drool drizzled down my chin as I pleasured him and then he pulled my head away. My mouth hung open and my gaze was still locked on his erection. I smiled as he pulled me down with him. I lay atop his body, draped over his muscles, feeling so small and petite compared to him. We kissed again, our tongues slipping and sliding against each other, our bodies sizzling with sweat in a hedonic mist. Our moans were loud, and I didn't care who could hear them. I wanted the world to know that our blood burned with the song of arousal, that our hearts were jubilant with the thrum of lust.

I could feel him pressing against me. He pushed me up so that my breasts were in his face. I could feel the pain of his teeth mix with the pleasure of his soft kisses. It was a potent cocktail that drove deep into the dwellings of my soul. But it wasn't enough.

"I need you," I whispered. His huge hands wrapped around my waist and forced me to straddle him. My legs widened and I found him, guiding him inside me effortlessly, as though he was always meant to be this close to me, as though we had always meant to be intimate. I winced as I felt him penetrate me. He was so thick that he stretched my tightness to its limit. He cradled my trembling body and then he started to thrust.

Fuck.

He hit the deepest part of me again and again, a part that no man had touched before. I felt like a virgin again it was so sweet and heavenly and raw at the same time. I was flooded with pleasure again and I went limp over him, only just about managing to keep my head up. But my hair was falling all over the place, and it was soon covering my mouth like a veil. He grabbed my ass and used all his strength and athleticism to screw me, pounding me again and again in this relentless rhythm that was never going to let up. I drowned in the expanse of his flesh as I felt his cock ruin me. His grunting breaths crashed against my ear, and I could feel the tension rising inside his body. He grabbed the back of my head and kissed me again, holding me in place as though I was bound to him. His hips thrust like pistons, hammering into my soul. Squeaking whimpers burst out of me with every thrust until there was nothing left, until there was nothing but him.

I felt his quaking tremors surge through me. Warmth came crashing in and it spread all over my body. All at once every part of me was seized with this absolute, ultimate bliss and I honestly thought I had died and gone to heaven.

Sweat streaked down me, as well as whatever else flowed out of my body. I was drained and delirious as I slipped off him, and I couldn't speak for a long while afterwards. I was shaking after how intense it was and I was glad he was there to hold my trembling body. The afterglow of sex took a long time to dissipate. My heart was frantic, and I thought it was going to leap out of my body. As for Harry, well, he just lay there with a dazed look in his eyes and gazed up at the ceiling, saying 'fuck' over and over again, as though he couldn't believe what the two of us had just done.

The truth is that I couldn't quite believe it either, but we had.

He looked down at me and smirked. His hair was a mess, but he had never looked better.

"So, that felt pretty real to me, right?"

I laughed and nodded, and then bowed my head. I kissed his chest lightly and snuggled into him, still amazed at how right it felt to be with him. I thought about the matter and knew that this had gone way beyond the realm of a fake relationship. I couldn't deny the feelings within my heart, nor could I deny the raw, intense passion we had shared. I had to face the truth; I had fallen in love with the last man I had ever expected to have these feelings for.

Chapter Seventeen

Angel

I awoke with the expectation that Harry would still be there, but the bed was empty. There was a warm shadow where his body had been, so he couldn't have been gone for long. I pushed myself into a sitting position at first, worried, but then I saw a note he'd left.

Gone to get us some breakfast. Last night was amazing. Can't wait for an amazing day.

I held the note close to my heart for it made me smile. I couldn't wipe the grin off my face, but my happiness soon turned to dismay when I glanced towards Jeri's bed. Usually, I would have shared something this joyous with her, but there was still a rift between us. She had been angry that I had chosen Harry as my fake boyfriend. I had no idea how she was going to feel about the fact that we were now in a real relationship. I wasn't even sure how I felt about it. I was excited of course, but it was still a little daunting. It was hard to escape the trauma of what had happened before.

The pleasure of the previous night lingered within me, and it put a spring in my step. I didn't want to waste any moments with Harry, and I didn't want to wait for him to get back. I wanted to run out across the Met and tell everyone that I was in love, and that it was wonderful. I quickly splashed some water on my face and pulled a baggy t-shirt over me, as well as some yoga shorts. I wasn't wearing make-up and I probably looked a right state, but I didn't care. As long as Harry thought I was beautiful that's all that mattered, and I wanted to surprise him. We had been pretending to be in a relationship all across campus for a little while now, but I wanted to announce it officially by leaping on him and kissing him wildly.

Holding the note close, I sprinted towards the café, laughing gaily. But as I approached something caused me to stop in my tracks. I saw Harry, but he wasn't alone. He was standing with another girl, and they seemed to be deep in conversation. I didn't recognize her, but she looked similar to me. She seemed upset about something. Then she wrapped her arms around Harry's neck and kissed him on the cheek. It was the kind of kiss that suggested they were more than friends, and if he was this close with someone why hadn't she come up in all the time we had spent together?

I tried not to think the worst, but it was impossible. I tried to tell myself that he couldn't be seeing anyone else because we had spent so much time together, but how could I know that for sure? I had spent my whole relationship with Tommy believing that he was a gentleman, was I just making the same mistake again?

The note fell from my hand as the color drained from my face. I staggered back to my room, unsure how to feel or what to believe. It felt as though my happiness had just been ripped away from me and trampled on. How could Harry do this to me? How could he do this after all we had shared, after last night? By the time I got back to my room, tears were in my eyes and I was questioning everything. I couldn't believe that he would actually do this. I couldn't believe that this was happening again. I had been so careful. I had been so guarded, but the moment I let that guard down, I was given a fatal blow.

And the worst thing of all is that I had nobody else to console me. Jeri should have been there, but I had driven her away too. I had lost everything and everyone and now I was alone. I pulled my knees into my chest and rocked back and forth as the tears came streaming down my cheeks. I had gone from the heights of exhilaration to the depths of despair all because I had been foolish enough to let myself fall in love again. Well, no more. It ended here. I wasn't going to let myself be prey to this vengeful and horrid emotion. I wasn't ever going to let myself be swayed by the sense of romance that was in the air. I had to be better than that. I had to be stronger.

Love could go fuck itself, and Harry could go fuck himself too.

Chapter Eighteen

Angel

Harry burst through the door carrying two coffees and a bag of donuts. "I hope you got my note. I thought we could celebrate in style. Last night was just... it was incredible, and I want this to be a new beginning for us, Angel. I know that we didn't really have a chance to talk about it last night, but I get the feeling you feel the same way I do. I don't think this is fake anymore. Nothing has ever felt this real to me and I want to make it official. I want you to be my girlfriend."

The smile on his face was wide. The words were ebullient. They poured out of his mouth in a sing song rhythm that I had been longing to hear. My heart should have leapt when he asked the question, and I should have jumped into his arms. But I just stayed there on the bed, staring into space. My voice was terse when I spoke to him, and I didn't dare look at him because I knew that I would just break down again. My body was ice and nausea swam in the pit of my stomach. I felt exactly the same way I did when I learned the truth about Tommy. Part of me just wanted Harry to leave. Another part wanted to scream and shout at him and make him pay for what he'd done. Another part of me just wanted to die.

"Who is she?" I asked.

Harry's expression changed immediately. "What?"

"The other girl. Who is she? Have you been dating her all this time or is it new?"

"I don't know what you're talking about Angel. What other girl? There is no other girl, there's only you. I thought I made that pretty clear last night."

Finally, I turned to face him. I stared daggers with him. "I just saw you with her, Harry. Don't try and deny it. I went to find you before you came back to surprise you and I saw you with her. Tell me who she is."

The look on Harry's face was priceless. It was the same look I'd seen before. That fake disbelief. That whirring of thoughts to try and conjure a lie that would rescue him from this situation.

"Angel, this isn't what you think it is. Please. You have to believe me. I meant everything I said last night. I've fallen in love with you. There's no way I'd want anyone else."

He spoke with such sincerity that it almost hurt my mind. I wish I could have believed him. I wish I could have trusted him, but I couldn't.

I stared at him with my bloodshot eyes. Sorrow poured out of me in tiny tears.

"I can't believe you, Harry. Not after everything that's happened. I saw you with her. You were clearly more than friends. I don't even care if you were breaking up with her so that you could be with me, the fact that there's another girl involved... I just can't take it. I can't believe after everything I've told you that you would do this. Maybe you're not so different from the way you used to be after all."

"I'm not like that, Angel. This isn't what you think. I promise you that. I'm not like Tommy. I'm not out to hurt you. I just want to be with you and to be happy. You should know this. Please. Why would I want to ruin this? I was lost before we started dating. You've made everything in my life better. My grades have improved, I actually feel like I belong here, I have something to look forward to. For the first time in my life, I feel like I can define myself as something other than Harry the hockey player, and I love it. I wouldn't want to jeopardize that."

"Then who was she? Why can't you tell me?" I asked, not understanding why he was still being so secretive about things.

"Angel, please, all I'm asking is that you trust me on this one thing. I won't ever ask you for anything for however long this relationship lasts. I just want this one single thing."

"I can't give it to you, Harry. I'm sorry. Maybe that's wrong of me, I don't know. Maybe I'm being selfish," the harsh words Jeri had said to me flashed through my mind. "But if you're not going to tell me who she was then I'm never going to be able to trust you properly. I might be asking too much, but if I'm going to be with someone, I need to know I'm with all of them. I can't be with you if you're going to hide a part of yourself from me because I'll always be wondering what's there and it's going to drive me crazy, so if you're not going to tell me then this might be it, as much as last night was amazing," I said, trying to hold back the sorrow from coming out in a flood. I hated how quickly things could turn from joy to despair. Only moments ago, I was soaring through the air, and now I was hating every moment of life.

"I don't want this to end, Angel. Please, you don't know what you're asking of me. You're asking me to break a promise..."

"It's just the way it has to be. If she's that important to you that you made a promise to her then clearly, she's special, so how am I supposed to think anything other than that you're in love with her?"

Harry stood there. I knew I was putting him in an impossible position, and I hated myself for it, but I couldn't ignore the feelings inside my heart. There was a stabbing sensation as all my fears swirled and collided with my heart, tearing away the slivers of hope I might have felt. Harry was so gorgeous and when I looked at him now, I couldn't help but think of his naked body pressing against mine, giving me so much pleasure. It was going to be sheer torture to excise that from my life, but I had to be ruthless when it came to protecting myself. He lifted his gaze to the ceiling and breathed deeply. I waited for him to leave, but he didn't.

"Okay," he said. "I'll tell you the truth."

Chapter Nineteen

Angel

Harry perched on the edge of the bed and rested his elbows on his knees, sitting forward and clasping his hands together. His voice was dry when he spoke, and I feared the worst. I sat there trembling, almost wishing that I hadn't asked for the truth because I was sure it was going to hurt.

"Her name is Mary," he began. "And she's not my girlfriend. In fact, she's not really anything to me. I've only ever met her once before."

"Then why did you two look so close?"

Harry pressed his lips together before he spoke again. "A few weeks ago, there was a party. It was a regular thing for us to do in between games. Some of the players liked to drink, but as you know I didn't. I went along for team bonding and because I liked the atmosphere, but I didn't take part in any of the drinking games or anything like that. Some guys bring friends and girlfriends and that sort of thing. It's a typical college party and there's never usually anything that special about them. Well, this night I noticed that there were a few guys surrounding this girl. Now the main guy here is Chase and I've never liked him. He's good on the ice, but he loves himself too much you know? Like he thinks he should be the star. Anyway, I noticed that she was getting drunker and drunker, and eventually the guys left with her in tow. Most of the other people were drunk, or they were distracted by other things so that they didn't notice. But I did, and it didn't seem right to me. It was late at night, so the campus was dark. I followed them but couldn't see them, but I heard some sounds coming from a dark area near one of the buildings. I got there and saw them, all over her, tearing at her clothes. She was clearly out of it, I mean, she was conscious, but her eyes were rolling in the back of her head, and she couldn't do anything to resist, especially not against these three guys. So, I yelled at them and charged, managed to pull them away and stood in between them. The guys were drunk, and they hadn't expected to be caught so they were off balance. I managed to fight them off and they ran away, and then I helped Mary back to her dorm."

"Wait, you saved a girl from being raped?" I asked, not entirely understanding the context of the situation.

"Pretty much, yeah."

"And that was her I just saw with you?"

Harry nodded. "It was. I'm sorry for not telling you about the truth before, but she wanted to keep the matter private. She didn't want her name being dragged around school because she knows what people are like. But she took some time away from college and she's decided that she's going to transfer. She came to pick up her stuff and she wanted to thank me and say goodbye, that's all. I promise you there wasn't anything more to it than that. I wanted to tell you the truth, believe me, but it wasn't my truth to give."

I sat there, stunned. "So, all this time you've had to put up with all these horrible rumors and people thinking that you did something wrong when actually you're kind of a hero?"

Harry shrugged. "I wasn't going to come out and say anything because people would only think I was saving my own skin, unless I actually said who the victim was. I didn't want to do that to Mary. She had enough to deal with anyway. So yeah, that was the price I paid, but I knew I did the right thing. But please, you can't tell anyone else about this."

I stared at him in wonder and feelings of guilt rushed through me as I knew I had been too hard on him. Here was a man who had sacrificed his own image and his own reputation and the sport he loved so much for the sake of protecting the dignity of a stranger. He was the complete opposite of Tommy and I hated myself for thinking the worst of him. But it didn't mean he should suffer like this.

"We have to tell someone. Hockey is your life. You shouldn't have to be kicked off the team because you stood up for someone who was in danger. This is wrong Harry. Can't you at least talk to your coach? We might even have to get the Dean involved. At least they'd be able to keep Mary's name out of it."

"It's not going to work Angel. They already know."

"What?" I gasped.

"I came into practice the next day and told Coach what had happened. Chase and the others were glaring at me. I knew it would hurt the team dynamics, but I had to tell Coach what had happened because I didn't want to be on the same team as rapists, and if they tried again with someone else then I'd be partly responsible. So, I spoke to Coach about it and said that I didn't want to reveal the name of the girl because of privacy issues and he said that he'd take the matter in hand. Then he spoke with the other guys and when he called me back into his office, he said that we had a bit of a situation because it was basically my word against theirs."

"What?!"

Harry nodded. "They said that they were taking Mary home because she had gotten too drunk, and she was feeling ill. They said that I had obviously misunderstood what was going on and had jumped to the wrong conclusion. Since there was no way to prove that my version of events was true without Mary coming out and saying anything, it stayed that way. I argued with Coach and told him that I couldn't play on the same team as these guys. He said that he wasn't going to ruin the dynamic of the team based on hearsay, and without proper evidence this couldn't go any further. He said that I should just drop the matter and get on with hockey because otherwise I'd be throwing away my career, but how could I play with them when I knew what kind of guys they were?"

"So, you just stopped?"

"No, then I went to the Dean and told him what was going on. He said he would take the matter very seriously, but in the end, he just agreed with Coach. He said that while the accusations were serious and while he didn't want this kind of thing happening in his college I had no hard evidence and they couldn't punish anyone based on what I said."

"Did you go to Mary again and ask her if she was willing to come forward?"

Harry shook his head. "After what they were like with me, I dreaded to think what they'd be like with her. I mean, she was so out of it, they'd be able to say that she was mistaken or something. I wasn't going to put her through that. I figured I'd just take the punches and be done with it. I didn't want to play hockey on that team with them anyway. And of course, it helps that Chase's parents are big sponsors here. I could have tried to take it further, but it would have only gotten me in more trouble. That's why I was so distant at the beginning. I'd just lost everything that was important to me, and nobody was willing to help. It didn't make sense really. In hockey, it's pretty much always the case that the best team wins, but that's not true in life."

"Were they the guys who beat you up?"

Harry nodded again. "They wanted to make sure that I wasn't going to tell anyone."

"Harry... that's awful," I said. Now the sorrow in my heart wasn't focused on myself, but on Harry. He had done the right thing and it had cost him everything, perhaps even his future. "I'm so sorry."

"It's okay, it's not like anyone can do anything about it. I'm just glad that I got there in time to stop them from hurting Mary."

"I mean I'm sorry about not trusting you. I'm sorry I'm such a mess," I said, turning away from him. He reached out and placed his hand under my chin, forcing me to look at him. He was smiling.

"Don't worry about it. I know it was hard for you to feel this way. There were so many times when I wanted to tell you the truth. I know I put on a brave face, but it has been hard to walk around knowing that everyone is staring at me and forming opinions of me based on rumor and hearsay. For a long time, all I wanted to do was shut myself away and not deal with the world at all. I wanted to tell Jeri as well of course. She was fighting so hard for me when I knew it was futile."

I nodded as he spoke. I had shut myself away because I had been scared of what might happen if I saw one man. Harry had done the same thing because he was afraid of the judgment of hundreds of people.

"I can't believe you stayed here. It would have been easier for you to go home."

"It would have been easier, yeah, and I did think about it, but that would only let them win. Besides, I had something to stick around for... you."

"Me?" I asked.

Harry grinned. "Yes, you," he chuckled lightly. "Angel, before we started dating, I was ready to shut myself away and be a recluse for the rest of my time at college. But then I remembered how fun life could be and I started to live in a way that I never had done before. My life has always revolved around hockey and while I've loved every minute of it, there's also a part of me that knows I've missed out on so much. You've shown me a glimpse of that, and I feel like a fool for waiting so long. I don't think you quite understand how much you mean to me. I feel like I can trust you with anything, and now that we're spending time together, the world doesn't seem bleak at all. I get excited about seeing you even if its just for a few moments, and I've never had this before. But I need you to accept that I'm not Tommy and I'm not setting out to hurt you. I know I was mean to you when we were younger, but we're not the same people, and you're not the same person that was hurt by Tommy either. You're better than that. You're better than him. We both deserve to be happy."

His words were strong, and I could feel them making my heart beat more fiercely. Our eyes locked and intense emotion poured out of me. I started weeping. I didn't know why. I wasn't even sad. Maybe it was out of relief. Maybe I just needed to get all this out of me. I had spent so long doubting everything, even Harry's feelings for me, but I couldn't do that any longer. I wanted to trust him. I wanted to love him. For the first time in what seemed like forever, I felt like I was capable of both these things. I flung my arms around him and for a long while we held each other like this. I clung to his sturdy body, knowing that he would never hurt me, while he held my trembling body, stopping me from utterly breaking apart.

Chapter Twenty

Angel

After a while Harry suggested we have a shower. I nodded. The night had been intense, and this conversation had left me with flushed cheeks and hair matted to my face. We walked to the shower and turned on the faucet. It didn't take long for the room to fill with steam. Harry and I stood next to each other. The previous night had been a moment of intense spontaneity, but this was more considered. Nerves now fluttered in my heart at the thought of being close with him again, even though I knew it was stupid because we had already made love. When I looked in his eyes, I felt at ease though, those kind eyes that were filled with compassion and love. I stroked his arms, and he took my hands, squeezing them softly. He leaned down and we kissed, and through this kiss, all of my nerves were dispelled. His hands fit naturally around my body, as though they were always meant to be there, and they always would be there. He caressed my neck and waist, smiling. I knew the same thoughts were going through his mind.

He reached down and whipped his top off, throwing it onto the floor. Soon enough all our clothes were in a puddle, unnecessary for what we had planned. We had only previously seen each other in the shadows of the night, so there was a moment where I was self-conscious about being naked in front of him with nowhere to hide the flaws of my body, but the way he looked set me at ease. He seemed as though he was in a dream. His lips were parted as he drank in every inch of me. His touch made me tingle, and I have to admit that I was sinking into the abyss of his body as well. My eyes lingered over every rippling muscle and followed the trail of dark hair down the middle of his stomach, loving everything that made him a man. I placed my hands on his chest and enjoyed the feeling of warmth that radiated from him.

He kissed me tenderly, placing a hand around the back of my head, supporting me as I rolled forward on my tiptoes. Then he led me into the shower. The water was warm, and it cascaded down us with all the freedom of a tidal wave. We giggled as we turned, and each had our moment under the water. Flecks of water dripped down my body. We were glistening as though we had been oiled by Greek gods. We held each other close and kissed deeply. I murmured with delight at the simple joy of being naked with him in this intimate way. The water was a comforting rhythm and it helped us shut out the rest of the world, as though we were hidden in our own secret pocket of the universe.

Harry's hands caressed my back and pressed me against the wall. The coolness of the tiles when compared with the warmth of the water was shocking, and I gasped. I giggled and flicked water at him, and we descended into laughter. Harry picked up some soap and we started to wash each other. Froth and foam lathered over our bodies, sliding against the slick surface of our flesh. My throat tightened as I ran my hands along the expanse of his body, washing him gently, becoming intimately familiar with every part of him. I took note of the places that made him laugh, those sweet spots that were only ever known by people who became so close.

He did the same thing with me. I loved the sight of his hands running over my stomach and around my body, touching me however he wanted. Once we were done washing, he kissed my neck and I felt tingles bloom and shiver down my body. A smile broadened on my face as I could feel his arousal pressing against me, and I knew that one night with him had definitely not been enough.

"Let's get dry," I whispered. The room was silent as the hissing stream of water was turned off, but the steam lingered. I pulled a towel off the rack, and we gently dried each other, gazing into each other's eyes the entire time. Our lips crashed against each other, and our bodies felt drawn to each other in an inexorable way. I couldn't quite understand it myself, this force that compelled us to be with each other, nor could I fight against it. I was about ready to drop to the floor then and make love with him wildly, but he guided me back to the bed. I stepped backwards, laughing as I felt as though I was going to teeter and fall, but Harry had his arms locked around my back, supporting me. There was no way he was going to allow me to fall.

At least that's what I thought, but then we reached the bed and he pushed me down. I yelped in surprise as I felt the world spinning and landed in the softness of the bed. Harry soon followed beside me. We were clean and fresh, smelling of lavender. It was as though we were in a meadow, rolling around with complete freedom. I wrapped my arms around him and pulled him close, kissing him deeply, wanting to share my body with him again. Now that I was with Harry, I remembered how powerful these sensations could be and how much I had denied myself since being with Tommy. He placed a hand on my hip and lay atop me, kissing me passionately. I let my hand linger against his back, feeling the tremors that rippled through his body and the almost imperceptible movements of every sinew as he moved.

His hand slithered down, passing along the rise of my breasts and then the depths of my flat stomach. His palm pressed flat against me, and I felt the tension growing inside before he found me, damp and sizzling with arousal. I murmured as my eyelids fluttered shut and the pleasure started to pour through my body. My neck arched as his fingers slid inside me, plunging into my most intimate area, the area that he was a master of. I could feel the curling motions, coaxing all the orgasmic feelings out of me. The night had been filled with this raw sense of unstoppable lust, but this second time was even better. We took time with each other, caressing each other and becoming familiar with all the valleys of our bodies. I loved the way he kissed my breasts as he played with me. His biceps tightened against my legs. I looked down and grinned at the way he toyed with me like a puppet, completely in control of every sensation that was careening through me. Sweat prickled all over and this made the shower we had taken completely redundant, but I didn't care. Pleasure cascaded through my entire body, and I found it hard to believe that it was caused by one single finger.

I wanted to kiss him, but I was too busy moaning. A knot untangled inside me and as I whispered my desire to him, he listened. He knew exactly what my body needed. The rhythm was unyielding, and he never stopped, not until the very end, not until everything shuddered out of me with the exquisite crack of a whip and I lay there, motionless and overwhelmed, but still greedy. He pulled his hand away from me and sat there, resting on his knees. I looked at him in all his glory and reached out, taking his erection in my hand. My fingers curled naturally around it and I moaned as I pleasured him stroking the skin back and forth, making him feel so good.

He came and lay beside me on his back. My head was still blistering from the echoes of pleasure. There was a dazed look in my eyes as I rolled over him and played with him, marveling at the sight of this huge tower standing so tall, this thick flesh that was alive with passion and lust, that now meant everything to me. I took my time to tease and torment him. I went slowly, ever so slowly, pulling back the skin until it was completely taut and then letting go. His erection slapped against his stomach before I caught it again and then went faster, my hand a blur. He loved this. I loved every small grunt and every terse moan that burst out of his mouth.

"Nobody has ever been this good before," he said, and his praise only made my confidence grow. I sucked him, just a little bit, just enough to let my saliva drizzle over him and then I jerked him off again, coating him in this wetness and fuck, it drove him crazy. His entire body shook as he placed a hand to his head in shock, moaning deeply, telling me that he was so close, ever so close, but I wasn't ready for him yet. I wanted him inside me.

I kissed him and lay on my back, pulling him over me. I wanted to feel him atop me, to feel him become my entire world. He cradled my head and I watched as he entered me, so huge, so thick, hitting the glorious, sweet spot between pain and pleasure that was always so elusive and always so rewarding. I gasped as every inch of him plunged inside me. He buried his head next to me as he started to thrust. Our bodies rocked and the bed creaked, and the world spun. I lost myself in him and he in me. I couldn't tell where I ended and he began, and this was the way love should be.

Errant kisses flashed across my mouth, but in truth we were moaning too fervently to make out for any real length of time. We were both breathless and needed to drink in as much air as we could. Raw pleasure rose within me again, bringing me to the brink of climax and then sending me tumbling over, as though I was plummeting through an endless abyss. My mind whirled and cracked with exhilaration as I clung to his body. Every toned muscle in him was focused on me, on giving me pleasure, as though he had been training for this his entire life. My legs curled around him and somehow, he got even deeper, as though he was touching my soul. I grabbed a handful of his short but thick hair, while his arms had wrapped around my body and cradled me tightly, cocooning myself in his entire essence. The air simmered with the heat we caused. Again and again, he thrust inside me, taking us closer to heaven. I whimpered and moaned, riding the sensations as they careened through me. I was completely at the mercy of them, as though I had been possessed by the essence of Eros, as though I was no longer myself.

Perhaps I wasn't.

I could feel all the worst parts of me being burned away by this passionate lust. The orgasmic blaze seared away my flaws. I was left a better person, breathless and drained.

The world shook as Harry neared his climax. I felt every quaking tremor in his body, every hard thrust that slammed into me and almost made me feel as though I was going to break in two, like a brittle twig.

When he came, it was with all the intensity he could muster. It burned inside me as hot as a supernova and as violent as a volcano. His body moved faster than what I thought was possible and I thought the world was going to crack underneath us, and then this feeling of bliss settled upon us like a fine mist. We lay there still and silent after so much heat and passion. Our chests heaved and I was entirely enchanted by the moment. A dazed look was upon my face as our bodies parted, but our souls were still entwined. We kissed lazily, barely having the strength to part our lips.

"I love you," I whispered.

"I love you too." He pressed his head against mine and we closed our eyes. I could see our future unspooling in my mind, and I wasn't scared about him hurting me or betraying me. I knew I could trust me. He had been my enemy once, but now he was my lover, and I wouldn't have had it any other way.

Chapter Twenty-One

Angel

When Harry and I made our relationship official nothing changed in the grand scheme of things because people around college thought we had been dating already, but I certainly looked at things with new eyes. The world seemed a little brighter and I glared at anyone who dared whisper as Harry and I passed. I wish I could have told them the truth because I hated how people still viewed him with suspicion or assumed that he had been the one to do something wrong, when actually he was the only person in the situation who had acted with courage and nobility. But that was the kind of man he was. I had always viewed him as a mean bully, but now that we were older, I realized that things were never that simple. I was glad to have been able to see his hidden depths. Nothing had ever been so beautiful to me.

Harry seemed to be in good spirits as well. He told me he didn't miss hockey, and while I didn't think he was lying to me, I did think he was lying to himself. I noticed the way he cast a lingering glance towards anything to do with hockey, and he always got tense before a game. I knew he wouldn't be able to stay away forever and that was okay. It had been something he had been training for his whole life, but at least now he knew there was more to life than being on the ice. I didn't think I had to worry about becoming a hockey widow as he made it clear that I meant more to him than that.

He also said something else that surprised me once as well. It came out of the blue one day. We hadn't reached the point where we were talking too specifically about the future, like kids and things. Those were cast in a hazy miasma that lingered on the horizon of our lives and I wasn't in particularly any rush to get there, but Harry remarked one day that when he had kids, he didn't want to push them into doing something like his parents had pushed him into hockey. It was a simple comment that was a part of a larger conversation, but it made me think about the future and I smiled with hope about what awaited us in the future. I had a feeling it was going to be glorious.

But unfortunately, not everything in our lives was happy. I had still lost my best friend and I wasn't sure how to get her back. Harry and I spoke about it often. In fact, in the first few days of our flourishing love Jeri was the main topic of conversation. We both felt as though we had let her down and that, if we hadn't been so concerned with our own problems, then perhaps she wouldn't have fallen prey to Tommy's charm. There was little we could do to save her either. She made it clear that she didn't want to see us, and anything we said against Tommy would only be seen as some desperate attack to prevent her from being happy. It was difficult to know that my friend was so misguided, especially when previously she had been so levelheaded.

But perhaps that had been part of the problem. I had always taken for granted the fact that she had been the reasonable one, when in reality, she was just a person with the same flaws as the rest of us. She had always been desperate for a boyfriend and Tommy had struck when she was at her most vulnerable. If I had been stronger, then I would have been with her and none of this would have happened. It was my fault that she was with Tommy, and I wracked my brains to try and think of a way to save her. Harry said that there wasn't anything we could do, because we couldn't force her away from something that she thought was making her happy, even though he hated the idea as well. I felt so powerless, and I hated how things had descended to such a point where Jeri was so desperately lonely, and I hadn't been able to tell.

There were occasions where I saw her across campus, always hanging off Tommy's arm. He looked happy, but Jeri looked haunted and pale. There were times when our eyes met. I smiled, hoping to close the distance that had formed between us, but she always tore her gaze away and whenever I went to approach her, she was gone, as though she was a phantom that had been lost in the shadows.

Thanks to my relationship with Harry, I was able to feel more confident and more level headed. I got back to my studies, and I helped Harry too. Our grades improved and I was confident that we would both succeed at college, and he started to believe that he might not need hockey after all.

The only cloud on our horizon was Jeri. My heart sank every time I thought of the way I had neglected her and taken her for granted as a friend, and I hated that it was too late to make amends. There were so many things I would have done differently had I had a chance, but I just had to hope that the day would come when she saw sense and realized that Tommy wasn't the guy she thought he was. However, I knew how difficult it was to escape that web. Even when I learned that he was cheating on me, there was a part of me that wanted to make it work.

*

One evening I was sitting alone studying, trying to wrap my head around a difficult paper that was going to make up a huge part of my grade, when there was a knock at the door. I chuckled to myself as I assumed that it was Harry coming to cheer me up. I'd told him how much I was struggling with this. I had also told him that I didn't want to be disturbed until I had cracked the paper, but he didn't always listen to me. I pulled myself up and was in the middle of laughing, ready to chastise him lightly for disturbing me, although I didn't really mean it. In fact, I would have welcomed the reaction, but when I opened the door I was shocked to find that it wasn't Harry standing there at all. It was Jeri.

"Do you mind if I come in?" she asked. Her voice was so soft it was almost a whisper. She looked down, seemingly unable to pick her gaze up off the floor, and she gnawed on her lower lip. Even though, technically, we still shared a room, it had been a while since she had been back here. She'd moved most of her stuff over to Tommy's dorm.

"Of course, Jeri," I said, opening the door wider so that she could enter. She shuffled in and looked at the familiar surroundings, before sighing as she sat on the bed.

"I missed this place," she said softly. I was unsure what she was doing here, but I didn't want to waste the opportunity. I spoke calmly in the hope that I wouldn't say anything to startle her or send her rushing away.

"I missed you. How are things?"

Jeri stared into space and then suddenly, she burst into tears. She held her head in her hands. Her shoulders shuddered and great wails poured out of her throat. All the tension that had risen between us vanished as I descended to her side and held her closely, just as she had comforted me so many times.

"It happened, Angel. You were right. He hadn't changed at all," she said.

"I'm sorry Jeri. I'm so sorry," I said, squeezing her tightly.

"I've been so stupid. I should have never gone out with him. I knew it was wrong in my head. I knew everything he had done to you, but I still let myself believe his lies. Oh God I'm such an idiot," she said in heaving breaths, shuddering between every other word.

"You're not an idiot Jeri. This is just what he does."

"I just thought he was the only guy who could ever love me. I thought if I didn't take a chance with him, then I was never going to be with anyone and I was so sick of being alone. I couldn't take it anymore."

"I know. It's not your fault. I'm sorry. I should have been a better friend. I took you for granted, Jeri. I'll never do that again. I should have been there for you when you were there for me, and I'm sorry that I wasn't. I'm sorry that I was so wrapped up in my own problems."

Jeri sniffed and shook her head. "It's not your fault. I was a real bitch. I just wanted things to change."

"How about we agree that we both weren't at our best and leave it at that," I said, reassuring her. It seemed to work. Jeri sniffed back her sadness and calmed down a bit. "So, what exactly happened?"

"Things were going well for a while. At first, I told myself that I had to be careful because of what happened to you, but when Tommy spoke about things from his point of view, he just made so much sense. And he showed such an interest in me, you know, that nobody else had before. I wanted to believe that it was real. But then, when things got on, I started noticing things about Tommy. He loved being around people and he always made them laugh, but he started to go out with these girls. At first, he told me that he was just friends with them, and then he said there was something more, but that it was okay because he was polyamorous and we could have an open relationship. He said that it was common these days and it didn't mean that he loved me any less, and he promised me that it wouldn't change how much time we spent together or anything like that, and he said that I could go out with other guys if I wanted to. But I didn't want to. I told myself that maybe, this was just the way things were, and I thought I could give it a chance. But then he started seeing me less and less and I overheard someone speaking about me, they said that I was a fool because I let him walk all over me and I just... I couldn't take it. I asked him whether we could go back to being a normal couple and he shouted at me. He yelled and said I should be grateful that he even bothered with me because nobody else did and then I just... then I just ran away, and I didn't have anywhere to go."

I listened to her story, horrified, but sadly I wasn't surprised that Tommy would do something like this.

"You know you always have somewhere to go, Jeri. I'm always here for you, no matter what," I said, squeezing her a little more tightly to emphasize my point. "And Harry is too."

She smiled at this. "Oh yeah, seems like you and he are getting on pretty well. Who would have thought you'd have fallen in love with my brother after you spent so long hating him?"

I blushed but smiled. "Yeah... well it took me by surprise as much as it did anyone else. You don't mind, do you? I mean, I guess it must be a little weird to know that your best friend and brother are dating."

Jeri wiped errant tears away from her eyes. "No, it's quite nice actually. All I've ever wanted is for the two of you to be happy, and if you can be happy together then that's more than I could ever ask for."

"Thanks, Jeri, and you'll be happy too. There's a guy out there for you, I promise there is, and one that will treat you better than Tommy. I didn't think there was for me, but then Harry turned up."

"I know, and I'll just have to be patient, but right now I just want to be back with you and Harry."

"Let's go and see him then," I said. Jeri nodded. We rose and walked arm in arm across the Met to Harry's dorm. As soon as he saw his sister, he realized what must have happened and he flung her arms around her in a tight embrace. The three of us were together again in a way that we had never been before. We were closer than ever.

We were a family.

*****

Don't miss out!

Visit the website below and you can sign up to receive emails whenever Erica Frost publishes a new book. There's no charge and no obligation.

https://books2read.com/r/B-A-YRSV-JUBEC

BOOKS2READ

Connecting independent readers to independent writers.

Also by Erica Frost

Seduced By A Billionaire
Dark Secrets
A Billionaire's Game
Power Play
Ruthless Rival
Taming The Billionaire
The Hated Billionaire
3-Pointer